Here's what kids have to say to
Mary Pope Osborne,
author of the Magic Tree House series:

Your books have gotten me interested in reading. That has made my parents very happy. —Philip J.

I wish I could keep all your books in a glass case with a golden key. —Luke R.

I love your Magic Tree House series. I even pretend that I am Jack. —Tommy C.

I'd like to be a writer just like you.—Meghan G.

Your books really make me dream.—Kurt K.

I think you are the best writer in all mankind! —Heather O.

I can't wait until that new book you're working on comes out. —Art N.

Your books are very, very, very, very good. I like them so much I'd buy them from you. —Patrick W.

I hope you come out with more than one hundred Jack and Annie books. They are the best books I ever read. If you had a subscription I bet there would be more than 500 people in it. —Brock G.

I am a big fan of your Magic Tree House books. —Nick O.

I love your books because they are funny and scary…Thank you for making reading fun! —Michael C.

…I love the Magic Tree House series. I can't wait till you write more books. —Asher M.

I like the Dinosaurs Before Dark *book. I like the girl. She was brave.* —Kellye

I like The Knight at Dawn. *I think it is a nice idea to make a Magic Tree House book. I think we will like the third book and if you make a fourth book we will like it too.* —Shane W.

Mrs. Bryant started to read Mummies in the Morning. *She said she was going to stop halfway through but we wouldn't let her because we were so interested in the book.* —Ashley E.

My favorite book is Pirates Past Noon. *I enjoy it because you tell who the magic person is.* —Ian

Write to Mary Pope Osborne yourself!
See page 303 for the address.

Magic Tree House

Collection #1

The Mystery of the Tree House

Look for these books by
Mary Pope Osborne!

Magic Tree House books:

Dinosaurs Before Dark (#1)
The Knight at Dawn (#2)
Mummies in the Morning (#3)
Pirates Past Noon (#4)
Night of the Ninjas (#5)
Afternoon on the Amazon (#6)
Sunset of the Sabertooth (#7)

Picture books:

Molly and the Prince
Moonhorse

For middle-grade readers:

American Tall Tales
Run, Run, as Fast as You Can
*Spider Kane and the Mystery at
   Jumbo Nightcrawler's*
*Spider Kane and the Mystery Under
   the May-Apple*

Magic Tree House

Collection #1

The Mystery of the Tree House

by Mary Pope Osborne

illustrated by Sal Murdocca

Random House 🏠 New York

Contents

Magic Tree House

Collection #1

The Mystery of the Tree House

Dinosaurs
Before Dark

For Linda and Mallory,
who took the trip with me

Contents

1

Into the Woods

"Help! A monster!" said Annie.

"Yeah, sure," said Jack. "A real monster in Frog Creek, Pennsylvania."

"Run, Jack!" said Annie. She ran up the road.

Oh, brother.

This is what he got for spending time with his seven-year-old sister.

Annie loved pretend stuff. But Jack was eight and a half. He liked *real* things.

"Watch out, Jack! The monster's coming! Race you!"

"No, thanks," said Jack.

Annie raced alone into the woods.

Jack looked at the sky. The sun was about to set.

"Come on, Annie! It's time to go home!"

But Annie had disappeared.

Jack waited.

No Annie.

"Annie!" he shouted again.

"Jack! Jack! Come here!"

Jack groaned. "This better be good," he said.

Jack left the road and headed into the woods. The trees were lit with a golden late-afternoon light.

"Come here!" called Annie.

There she was. Standing under a tall oak tree. "Look," she said. She was pointing at a rope ladder.

The longest rope ladder Jack had ever seen.

"Wow," he whispered.

The ladder went all the way up to the top of the tree.

There—at the top—was a tree house. It was tucked between two branches.

"That must be the highest tree house in the world," said Annie.

"Who built it?" asked Jack. "I've never seen it before."

"I don't know. But I'm going up," said Annie.

"No. We don't know who it belongs to," said Jack.

"Just for a teeny minute," said Annie. She started up the ladder.

"Annie, come back!"

She kept climbing.

Jack sighed. "Annie, it's almost dark. We have to go home."

Annie disappeared inside the tree house.

"An-nie!"

Jack waited a moment. He was about to call again when Annie poked her head out of the tree house window.

"Books!" she shouted.

"What?"

"It's filled with books!"

Oh, man! Jack loved books.

He pushed his glasses into place. He gripped the sides of the rope ladder, and up he went.

2

The Monster

Jack crawled through a hole in the tree house floor.

Wow. The tree house *was* filled with books. Books everywhere. Very old books with dusty covers. New books with shiny, bright covers.

"Look. You can see far, far away," said Annie. She was peering out the tree house window.

Jack looked out the window with her. Down below were the tops of the other trees. In the distance he saw the Frog Creek library.

The elementary school. The park.

Annie pointed in the other direction.

"There's our house," she said.

Sure enough. There was their white wooden house with the green porch. Next door was their neighbor's black dog, Henry. He looked very tiny.

"Hi, Henry!" shouted Annie.

"Shush!" said Jack. "We're not supposed to be up here."

He glanced around the tree house again.

"I wonder who owns all these books," he said. He noticed bookmarks were sticking out of many of them.

"I like this one," said Annie. She held up a book with a castle on the cover.

"Here's a book about Pennsylvania," said Jack. He turned to the page with the bookmark.

13

"Hey, there's a picture of Frog Creek in here," said Jack. "It's a picture of *these* woods!"

"Oh, here's a book for you," said Annie. She held up a book about dinosaurs. A blue silk bookmark was sticking out of it.

"Let me see it." Jack set down his backpack and grabbed the book from her.

"You look at that one, and I'll look at the one about castles," said Annie.

"No, we better not," said Jack. "We don't know who these books belong to."

But even as he said this, Jack opened the dinosaur book to where the bookmark was. He couldn't help himself.

He turned to a picture of an ancient flying reptile. A Pteranodon.

He touched the huge bat-like wings.

"Wow," whispered Jack. "I wish I could

14

see a Pteranodon for real."

Jack studied the picture of the odd-looking creature soaring through the sky.

"Ahhh!" screamed Annie.

"What?" said Jack.

"A monster!" Annie cried. She pointed to the tree house window.

"Stop pretending, Annie," said Jack.

"No, really!" said Annie.

Jack looked out the window.

A giant creature was gliding above the treetops! He had a long, weird crest on the back of his head. A skinny beak. And huge bat-like wings!

It was a real live Pteranodon!

The creature curved through the sky. He was coming straight toward the tree house. He looked like a glider plane!

The wind began to blow.

The leaves trembled.

Suddenly the creature soared up. High into the sky. Jack nearly fell out the window trying to see it.

The wind picked up. It was whistling now.
The tree house started to spin.
"What's happening?" cried Jack.
"Get down!" shouted Annie.

She pulled him back from the window.

The tree house was spinning. Faster and faster.

Jack squeezed his eyes shut. He held on to Annie.

Then everything was still.

Absolutely still.

Jack opened his eyes. Sunlight slanted through the window.

There was Annie. The books. His backpack.

The tree house was still high up in an oak tree.

But it wasn't the *same* oak tree.

3

Where Is Here?

Jack looked out the window.

He looked down at the picture in the book.

He looked back out the window.

The world outside and the world in the picture—they were exactly the same.

The Pteranodon was soaring through the sky. The ground was covered with ferns and tall grass. There was a winding stream. A sloping hill. And volcanoes in the distance.

"Wh—where are we?" stammered Jack.

The Pteranodon glided down to the base of their tree. The creature coasted to a stop. And stood very still.

"What happened to us?" said Annie. She looked at Jack. He looked at her.

"I don't know," said Jack. "I was looking at the picture in the book—"

"And you said, 'Wow, I wish I could see a Pteranodon for real,' " said Annie.

"Yeah. And then we saw one. In the Frog Creek woods," said Jack.

"Yeah. And then the wind got loud. And the tree house started spinning," said Annie.

"And we landed here," said Jack.

"And we landed here," said Annie.

"So that means . . ." said Jack.

"So that means . . . what?" said Annie.

"Nothing," said Jack. He shook his head. "None of this can be real."

Annie looked out the window again. "But *he*'s real," she said. "He's *very* real."

Jack looked out the window with her. The Pteranodon was standing at the base of the oak tree. Like a guard. His giant wings were spread out on either side of him.

"Hi!" Annie shouted.

"Shush!" said Jack. "We're not supposed to be here."

"But where is *here?*" said Annie.

"I don't know," said Jack.

"Hi!" Annie called again to the creature.

The Pteranodon looked up at them.

"Where is *here?*" Annie called down.

"You're nuts. He can't talk," said Jack. "But maybe the book can tell us."

Jack looked down at the book. He read the words under the picture:

> **This flying reptile lived in the Cretaceous period. It vanished 65 million years ago.**

No. Impossible. They couldn't have landed in a time 65 million years ago.

"Jack," said Annie. "He's nice."

"Nice?"

"Yeah, I can tell. Let's go down and talk to him."

"Talk to him?"

Annie started down the rope ladder.

"Hey!" shouted Jack.

But Annie kept going.

"Are you crazy?" Jack called.

Annie dropped to the ground. She stepped boldly up to the ancient creature.

4

Henry

Jack gasped as Annie held out her hand.

Oh, brother. She was always trying to make friends with animals. But this was going too far.

"Don't get too close to him, Annie!" Jack shouted.

But Annie touched the Pteranodon's crest. She stroked his neck. She was talking to him.

What in the world was she saying?

Jack took a deep breath. Okay. He would go down too. It would be good to examine the creature. Take notes. Like a scientist.

Jack started down the rope ladder.

When he got to the ground, Jack was only a few feet away from the creature.

The creature stared at Jack. His eyes were bright and alert.

"He's soft, Jack," said Annie. "He feels like Henry."

Jack snorted. "He's no dog, Annie."

"Feel him, Jack," said Annie.

Jack didn't move.

"Don't think, Jack. Just do it."

Jack stepped forward. He put out his arm. Very cautiously. He brushed his hand down the creature's neck.

Interesting. A thin layer of fuzz covered the Pteranodon's skin.

"Soft, huh?" said Annie.

Jack reached into his backpack and pulled

out a pencil and a notebook. He wrote:

fuzzy skin

"What are you doing?" asked Annie.

"Taking notes," said Jack. "We're probably the first people in the whole world to ever see a real live Pteranodon."

Jack looked at the Pteranodon again. The creature had a bony crest on top of his head. The crest was longer than Jack's arm.

"I wonder how smart he is," Jack said.

"*Very* smart," said Annie.

"Don't count on it," said Jack. "His brain's probably no bigger than a bean."

"No, he's very smart. I can feel it," said Annie. "I'm going to call him Henry."

Jack wrote in his notebook:

small brain?

Jack looked at the creature again. "Maybe he's a mutant," he said.

The creature tilted his head.

Annie laughed. "He's no mutant, Jack."

"Well, what's he doing here then? Where is this place?" said Jack.

Annie leaned close to the Pteranodon.

"Do you know where we are, Henry?" she asked softly.

The creature fixed his eyes on Annie. His long jaws were opening and closing. Like a giant pair of scissors.

"Are you trying to talk to me, Henry?" asked Annie.

"Forget it, Annie." Jack wrote in his notebook:

mouth like scissors?

"Did we come to a time long ago, Henry?"

asked Annie. "Is this a place from long ago?" Suddenly she gasped. "Jack!"

He looked up.

Annie was pointing toward the hill. On top stood a huge dinosaur!

5

Gold in the Grass

"Go! *Go!*" said Jack. He threw his notebook into his pack. He pushed Annie toward the rope ladder.

"Bye, Henry!" she said.

"Go!" said Jack. He gave Annie a big push.

"Quit it!" she said. But she started up the ladder. Jack scrambled after her.

They tumbled into the tree house.

They were panting as they looked out the window at the dinosaur. He was standing on the hilltop. Eating flowers off a tree.

"Oh, man," whispered Jack. "We *are* in a time long ago!"

The dinosaur looked like a huge rhinoceros. Only he had three horns instead of one. Two long ones above his eyes and one on his nose. He had a big shield-like thing behind his head.

"Triceratops!" said Jack.

"Does he eat people?" whispered Annie.

"I'll look it up." Jack grabbed the dinosaur book. He flipped through the pages.

"There!" he said. He pointed to a picture of a Triceratops. He read the caption:

> **The Triceratops lived in the late Cretaceous period. This plant-eating dinosaur weighed over 12,000 pounds.**

Jack slammed the book shut. "Just plants. No meat."

"Let's go see him," said Annie.

"Are you nuts?" said Jack.

"Don't you want to take notes about him?" asked Annie. "We're probably the first people in the whole world to ever see a real live Triceratops."

Jack sighed. She was right.

"Let's go," he said.

He shoved the dinosaur book into his pack. He slung it over his shoulder and started down the ladder.

On the way down, Jack stopped.

He called up to Annie, "Just promise you won't pet him."

"I promise."

"Promise you won't kiss him."

"I promise."

"Promise you won't talk to him."

"I promise."

"Promise you won't—"

"Go! Go!" she said.

Jack went.

Annie followed.

When they stepped off the ladder, the Pteranodon gave them a kind look.

Annie blew a kiss at him. "Be back soon, Henry," she said cheerfully.

"Shush!" said Jack. And he led the way through the ferns. Slowly and carefully.

When he reached the bottom of the hill, he kneeled behind a fat bush.

Annie knelt beside him and started to speak.

"Shush!" Jack put his finger to his lips.

Annie made a face.

Jack peeked out at the Triceratops.

The dinosaur was incredibly big. Bigger than a truck. He was eating the flowers off a magnolia tree.

Jack slipped his notebook out of his pack. He wrote:

eats flowers

Annie nudged him.

Jack ignored her. He studied the Triceratops again. He wrote:

eats slowly

Annie nudged him hard.

Jack looked at her.

Annie pointed to herself. She walked her fingers through the air. She pointed to the dinosaur. She smiled.

Was she teasing?

She waved at Jack.

Jack started to grab her.

She laughed and jumped away. She fell into the grass. In full view of the Triceratops!

"Get back!" whispered Jack.

Too late. The big dinosaur had spotted Annie. He gazed down at her from the hilltop. Half of a magnolia flower was sticking out of his mouth.

"Oops," said Annie.

"Get back!" Jack shouted at her.

"He looks nice, Jack."

"Nice? Watch out for his horns, Annie!"

"No. He's nice, Jack."

Nice?

But the Triceratops just gazed calmly down at Annie. Then he turned and loped away. Down the side of the hill.

"Bye!" said Annie. She turned back to Jack. "See?"

Jack grunted. But he wrote in his notebook:

nice

"Come on. Let's look around some more,"
said Annie.

As Jack started after Annie, he saw something glittering in the tall grass. He reached
out and picked it up.

A medallion. A gold medallion.

A letter was engraved on the medallion. A fancy M.

"Oh, man. Someone came here before us," Jack said softly.

6

Dinosaur Valley

"Annie, look at this!" Jack called. "Look what I found!"

Annie had gone up to the hilltop.

She was busy picking a flower from the magnolia tree.

"Annie, look! A medallion!"

But Annie wasn't paying attention to Jack. She was staring at something on the other side of the hill.

"Oh, wow!" she said.

"Annie!"

Clutching her magnolia flower, she took off down the hill.

"Annie, come back!" Jack shouted.

But Annie had disappeared.

"I'm going to kill her," Jack muttered.

He stuffed the gold medallion into his jeans pocket.

Then he heard Annie shriek.

"Annie?"

Jack heard another sound as well. A deep, bellowing sound. Like a tuba.

"Jack! Come here!" Annie called.

"Annie!"

Jack grabbed his backpack and raced up the hill.

When he got to the top, he gasped.

The valley below was filled with nests. Big nests made out of mud. And the nests were filled with tiny dinosaurs!

Annie was crouching next to one of the nests. And standing over her was a gigantic duck-billed dinosaur!

"Don't panic. Don't move," said Jack. He stepped slowly down the hill toward Annie.

The huge dinosaur was towering above Annie. Waving her arms. Making her tuba sound.

Jack stopped. He didn't want to get too close.

He knelt on the ground. "Okay. Move toward me. Slowly," he said.

Annie started to stand up.

"Don't stand. Crawl," said Jack.

Clutching her flower, Annie crawled toward Jack.

The duck-billed dinosaur followed her. Still bellowing.

Annie froze.

"Keep going," Jack said softly.

Annie started crawling again.

Jack inched farther down the hill. Until he was just an arm's distance from Annie.

He reached out—and grabbed her hand.

He pulled Annie toward him.

"Stay down," he said. He crouched next to her. "Bow your head. Pretend to chew."

"Chew?"

"Yes. I read that's what you do if a mean dog comes at you."

"She's no dog, Jack," said Annie.

"Just chew," said Jack.

Jack and Annie both bowed their heads. And pretended to chew.

Soon the dinosaur grew quiet.

Jack raised his head.

"I don't think she's mad anymore," he said.

"Thanks, Jack, for saving me," said Annie.

"You have to use your brain," said Jack. "You can't just go running to a nest of babies. There's always a mother nearby."

Annie stood up.

"Annie!"

Too late.

Annie held out her magnolia flower to the dinosaur.

"I'm sorry I made you worry about your babies," she said.

The dinosaur moved closer to Annie. She grabbed the flower from her. She reached for another.

"No more," said Annie.

The dinosaur let out a sad tuba sound.

"But there are more flowers up there," Annie said. She pointed to the top of the hill. "I'll get you some."

Annie hurried up the hill.

The dinosaur waddled after her.

Jack quickly examined the babies. Some were crawling out of their nests.

Where were the other mothers?

Jack took out the dinosaur book. He flipped through the pages.

He found a picture of some duck-billed dinosaurs. He read the caption:

> **The Anatosauruses lived in colonies. While a few mothers baby-sat the nests, others hunted for food.**

So there must be more mothers close by.

"Hey, Jack!" Annie called.

Jack looked up. Annie was at the top of the hill. Feeding magnolia flowers to the giant Anatosaurus!

"She's nice, too, Jack," Annie said.

But suddenly the Anatosaurus made her

terrible tuba sound. Annie crouched down and started to chew.

The dinosaur barged down the hill.

She seemed afraid of something.

Jack put the book down on top of his pack.

He hurried up to Annie.

"I wonder why she ran away," said Annie. "We were starting to be friends."

Jack looked around. What he saw in the distance almost made him throw up.

An enormous ugly monster was coming across the plain.

He was walking on two big legs. And swinging a long, thick tail. And dangling two tiny arms.

He had a huge head. And his jaws were wide open.

Even from far away Jack could see his long, gleaming teeth.

"Tyrannosaurus rex!" whispered Jack.

7

Ready, Set, Go!

"Run, Annie! Run!" cried Jack. "To the tree house!"

They dashed down the hill together. Through the tall grass, through the ferns, past the Pteranodon, and right to the rope ladder.

They scrambled up. Seconds later they tumbled into the tree house.

Annie leaped to the window.

"He's going away!" she said, panting.

Jack pushed his glasses into place. He looked through the window with her.

49

The Tyrannosaurus was wandering off.

But then the monster stopped and turned around.

"Duck!" said Jack.

The two of them hunched down.

After a long moment, they raised their heads. They peeked out again.

"Coast clear," said Jack.

"Yay," whispered Annie.

"We have to get out of here," said Jack.

"You made a wish before," said Annie.

"I wish we could go back to Frog Creek," said Jack.

Nothing happened.

"I wish—"

"Wait. You were looking at a picture in the dinosaur book. Remember?"

The dinosaur book.

Jack groaned. "Oh, no. I left the book and

my pack on the hill. I have to go back."

"Oh, forget it," said Annie.

"I can't," said Jack. "The book doesn't belong to us. Plus my notebook's in my pack. With all my notes."

"Hurry!" said Annie.

Jack hurried down the rope ladder.

He leaped to the ground.

He raced past the Pteranodon, through the ferns, through the tall grass, and up the hill.

He looked down.

There was his pack, lying on the ground. On top of it was the dinosaur book.

But now the valley below was filled with Anatosauruses. All standing guard around the nests.

Where had they been? Did fear of the Tyrannosaurus send them home?

Jack took a deep breath.

Ready! Set! Go!

He charged down the hill. He leaped to his backpack. He scooped it up. He grabbed the dinosaur book.

A terrible tuba sound! Another! Another! All the Anatosauruses were bellowing at him.

Jack took off.

He raced up to the hilltop.

He started down the hill.

He stopped.

The Tyrannosaurus rex was back! And he was standing between Jack and the tree house!

8

A Giant Shadow

Jack jumped behind the magnolia tree.

His heart was beating so fast he could hardly think.

He peeked out at the giant monster. The horrible-looking creature was opening and closing his huge jaws. His teeth were as big as steak knives.

Don't panic. Think.

Jack peered down at the valley.

Good. The duck-billed dinosaurs were sticking close to their nests.

Jack looked back at the Tyrannosaurus.

Good. The monster still didn't seem to know he was there.

Don't panic. Think. *Think*. Maybe there's information in the book.

Jack opened the dinosaur book. He found Tyrannosaurus rex. He read:

> **Tyrannosaurus rex was the largest**
> **meat-eating land animal of all time.**
> **If it were alive today, it would eat a**
> **human in one bite.**

Great. The book was no help at all.

Okay. He couldn't hide on the other side of the hill. The Anatosauruses might stampede.

Okay. He couldn't run to the tree house. The Tyrannosaurus might run faster.

Okay. Maybe he should just wait. Wait for the monster to leave.

Jack peeked around the tree.

The Tyrannosaurus had wandered *closer* to the hill.

Something caught Jack's eye. Annie was coming down the rope ladder!

Was she nuts? What was she doing?

Jack watched Annie hop off the ladder.

She went straight to the Pteranodon. She was talking to him. She was flapping her arms. She pointed at Jack, at the sky, at the tree house.

She *was* nuts!

"Go! Go back up the tree!" Jack whispered. "Go!"

Suddenly Jack heard a roar.

The Tyrannosaurus rex was looking in his direction.

Jack hit the ground.

The Tyrannosaurus rex was coming toward the hill.

Jack felt the ground shaking.

Should he run? Crawl back into Dinosaur Valley? Climb the magnolia tree?

Just then a giant shadow covered Jack. He looked up.

The Pteranodon was gliding overhead. The giant creature sailed down toward the top of the hill.

He was coming straight for Jack.

9

The Amazing Ride

The Pteranodon coasted down to the ground.

He stared at Jack with his bright, alert eyes.

What was Jack supposed to do? Climb on? "But I'm too heavy," thought Jack.

Don't think. Just do it.

Jack looked at the Tyrannosaurus.

He was starting up the hill. His giant teeth were flashing in the sunlight.

Okay. Don't think. Just do it!

Jack put his book in his pack. Then he eased down onto the Pteranodon's back.

He held on tightly.

The creature moved forward. He spread out his wings—and lifted off the ground!

They teetered this way. Then that.

Jack nearly fell off.

The Pteranodon steadied himself, then rose into the sky.

Jack looked down. The Tyrannosaurus was chomping the air and staring up at him.

The Pteranodon glided away.

He sailed over the hilltop.

He circled over the valley. Over all the nests filled with babies. Over all the giant duck-billed dinosaurs.

Then the Pteranodon soared out over the plain—over the Triceratops who was grazing in the high grass.

It was amazing! It was a miracle!

Jack felt like a bird. As light as a feather.

The wind was rushing through his hair. The air smelled sweet and fresh.

He whooped. He laughed.

Jack couldn't believe it. He was riding on the back of an ancient flying reptile!

The Pteranodon sailed over the stream, over the ferns and bushes.

Then he carried Jack down to the base of the oak tree.

When they came to a stop, Jack slid off the creature's back. And landed on the ground.

Then the Pteranodon took off again and glided into the sky.

"Bye, Henry," whispered Jack.

"Are you okay?" Annie shouted from the tree house.

Jack pushed his glasses into place. He kept staring up at the Pteranodon.

"Jack, are you okay?" Annie called.

Jack looked up at Annie. He smiled.

"Thanks for saving my life," he said. "That was really fun."

"Climb up!" said Annie.

Jack tried to stand. His legs were wobbly.

He felt a bit dizzy.

"Hurry!" shouted Annie. "He's coming!"

Jack looked around. The Tyrannosaurus was heading straight toward him!

Jack bolted to the ladder. He grabbed the sides and started up.

"Hurry! Hurry!" screamed Annie.

Jack scrambled into the tree house.

"He's coming toward the tree!" Annie cried.

Suddenly something slammed against the oak tree. The tree house shook like a leaf.

Jack and Annie tumbled into the books.

"Make a wish!" cried Annie.

"We need the book! The one with the picture of Frog Creek!" said Jack. "Where is it?"

He pushed some books aside. He had to find that book about Pennsylvania.

There it was!

He grabbed it and tore through it, looking for the photograph of the Frog Creek woods.

He found it! Jack pointed to the picture.

"I wish we could go home!" he shouted.

The wind began to moan. Softly at first.

"Hurry!" Jack yelled.

The wind picked up. It was whistling now.

The tree house started to spin.

It spun faster and faster.

Jack closed his eyes. He held on tightly to Annie.

Then everything was still.

Absolutely still.

10

Home Before Dark

A bird began to sing.

Jack opened his eyes. He was still pointing at the picture of the Frog Creek woods.

He peeked out the tree house window. Outside he saw the exact same view.

"We're home," whispered Annie.

The woods were lit with a golden late-afternoon light. The sun was about to set.

No time had passed since they'd left.

"Ja-ack! An-nie!" a voice called from the distance.

"That's Mom," said Annie, pointing.

Jack saw their mother far away. She was
standing in front of their house. She looked
very tiny.

"An-nie! Ja-ack!" she called.

Annie stuck her head out the window and shouted, "Come-ing!"

Jack still felt dazed. He just stared at Annie.

"What happened to us?" he said.

"We took a trip in a magic tree house," said Annie simply.

"But it's the same time as when we left," said Jack.

Annie shrugged.

"And how did it take us so far away?" said Jack. "And so long ago?"

"You just looked at a book and said you wished we could go there," said Annie. "And the magic tree house took us there."

"But *how?*" said Jack. "And who built this magic tree house? Who put all these books here?"

"A magic person, I guess," said Annie.

A magic person?

"Oh, look," said Jack. "I almost forgot about this." He reached into his pocket and pulled out the gold medallion. "Someone lost this back there . . . in dinosaur land. Look, there's a letter M on it."

Annie's eyes got round. "You think *M* stands for *magic person?*" she said.

"I don't know," said Jack. "I just know someone went to that place before us."

"Ja-ack! An-nie!" came the distant cry again.

Annie poked her head out the window. "Come-ing!" she shouted.

Jack put the gold medallion back in his pocket.

He pulled the dinosaur book out of his pack. And put it back with all the other books.

Then he and Annie took one last look around the tree house.

"Good-bye, house," whispered Annie.

Jack slung his backpack over his shoulder. He pointed at the ladder.

Annie started down. Jack followed.

Seconds later they hopped onto the ground and started walking out of the woods.

"No one's going to believe our story," said Jack.

"So let's not tell anyone," said Annie.

"Dad won't believe it," said Jack.

"He'll say it was a dream," said Annie.

"Mom won't believe it," said Jack.

"She'll say it was pretend," said Annie.

"My teacher won't believe it," said Jack.

"She'll say you're nuts," said Annie.

"We better not tell anyone," said Jack.

"I already said that," said Annie.

Jack sighed. "I think I'm starting to not believe it myself," he said.

They left the woods and started up the road toward their house.

As they walked past all the houses on their street, the trip to dinosaur time *did* seem more and more like a dream.

Only *this* world and *this* time seemed real.

Jack reached into his pocket. He clasped the gold medallion.

He felt the engraving of the letter M. It made Jack's fingers tingle.

Jack laughed. Suddenly he felt very happy.

He couldn't explain what had happened today. But he knew for sure that their trip in the magic tree house had been real.

Absolutely real.

"Tomorrow," Jack said softly, "we'll go back to the woods."

"Of course," said Annie.

"And we'll climb up to the tree house," said Jack.

"Of course," said Annie.

"And we'll see what happens next," said Jack.

"Of course," said Annie. "Race you!"

And they took off together, running for home.

The Knight
at Dawn

For Nathaniel Pope

Contents

1

The Dark Woods

Jack couldn't sleep.

He put his glasses on. He looked at the clock. 5:30.

Too early to get up.

Yesterday so many strange things had happened. Now he was trying to figure them out.

He turned on the light. He picked up his notebook. He looked at the list he'd made before going to bed.

found tree house in woods
found lots of books in it
pointed to Pteranodon picture in book
made a wish
went to time of dinosaurs
pointed to picture of Frog Creek woods
made a wish
Came home to Frog Creek.

Jack pushed his glasses into place. Who was going to believe any of this?

Not his mom. Or his dad. Or his third-grade teacher, Ms. Watkins. Only his seven-year-old sister, Annie. She'd gone with him to the time of the dinosaurs.

"Can't you sleep?"

It was Annie, standing in his doorway.

"Nope," said Jack.

"Me neither," said Annie. "What are you doing?"

She walked over to Jack and looked at his notebook. She read the list.

"Aren't you going to write about the gold medal?" she asked.

"You mean the gold medallion," said Jack.

He picked up his pencil and wrote:

found this in dinosaur time

"Aren't you going to put the letter M on the medal?" said Annie.

"Medallion," said Jack. "Not medal."

He added an M:

"Aren't you going to write about the magic person?" said Annie.

"We don't know for sure if there is a magic person," said Jack.

"Well, someone built the tree house in the woods. Someone put the books in it. Someone lost a gold medal in dinosaur time."

"Medallion!" said Jack for the third time. "And I'm just writing the facts. The stuff we know for sure."

"Let's go back to the tree house right now," said Annie. "And find out if the magic person is a fact."

"Are you nuts?" said Jack. "The sun's not even up yet."

"Come on," said Annie. "Maybe we can catch them sleeping."

"I don't think we should," said Jack. He was worried. What if the "magic person" was

86

mean? What if he or she didn't want kids to know about the tree house?

"Well, I'm going," said Annie.

Jack looked out his window at the dark-gray sky. It was almost dawn.

He sighed. "Okay. Let's get dressed. I'll meet you at the back door. Be quiet."

"Yay!" whispered Annie. She tiptoed away as quietly as a mouse.

Jack put on jeans, a warm sweatshirt, and sneakers. He tossed his notebook and pencil in his backpack.

He crept downstairs.

Annie was waiting by the back door. She shined a flashlight in Jack's face. "Ta-da! A magic wand!" she said.

"Shhh! Don't wake up Mom and Dad," whispered Jack. "And turn that flashlight off. We don't want anyone to see us."

Annie nodded and turned it off. Then she clipped it onto her belt.

They slipped out the door into the cool early-morning air. Crickets were chirping. The dog next door barked.

"Quiet, Henry!" whispered Annie.

Henry stopped barking. Animals always seemed to do what Annie said.

"Let's run!" said Jack.

They dashed across the dark, wet lawn and didn't stop until they reached the woods.

"We need the flashlight now," said Jack.

Annie took it off her belt and switched it on.

Step by step, she and Jack walked between the trees. Jack held his breath. The dark woods were scary.

"Gotcha!" said Annie, shining the flashlight in Jack's face.

Jack jumped back. Then he frowned.

"Cut it out!" he said.

"I scared you," said Annie.

Jack glared at her.

"Stop pretending!" he whispered. "This is serious."

"Okay, okay."

Annie shined her flashlight over the tops of the trees.

"Now what are you doing?" said Jack.

"Looking for the tree house!"

The light stopped moving.

There it was. The mysterious tree house. At the top of the tallest tree in the woods.

Annie shined her light at the tree house, and then down the tall ladder. All the way to the ground.

"I'm going up," she said. She gripped the flashlight and began to climb.

"Wait!" Jack called.

What if someone was in the tree house?

"Annie! Come back!"

But she was gone. The light disappeared.
Jack was alone in the dark.

2

Leaving Again

"No one's here!" Annie shouted down.

Jack thought about going home. Then he thought about all the books in the tree house.

He started up the ladder. When he was nearly to the tree house, he saw light in the distant sky. Dawn was starting to break.

He crawled through a hole in the floor and took off his backpack.

It was dark inside the tree house.

Annie was shining her flashlight on the books scattered about.

"They're still here," she said.

She stopped the light on a dinosaur book. It was the book that had taken them to the time of the dinosaurs.

"Remember the Tyrannosaurus?" asked Annie.

Jack shuddered. Of course he remembered! How could anyone forget seeing a real live Tyrannosaurus rex?

The light fell on a book about Pennsylvania. A red silk bookmark stuck out of it.

"Remember the picture of Frog Creek?" said Annie.

"Of course," said Jack. That was the picture that had brought them home.

"There's my favorite," said Annie.

The light was shining on a book about knights and castles. There was a blue leather bookmark in it.

Annie turned to the page with the bookmark. There was a picture of a knight on a black horse. He was riding toward a castle.

"Annie, close that book," said Jack. "I know what you're thinking."

Annie pointed at the knight.

"Don't, Annie!"

"We wish we could see this guy for real," Annie said.

"No, we don't!" shouted Jack.

They heard a strange sound.

"*Neeee-hhhh!*"

It sounded like a horse neighing.

They both went to the window.

Annie shined the flashlight down on the ground.

"Oh no," whispered Jack.

"A knight!" said Annie.

A knight in shining armor! Riding a black horse! Through the Frog Creek woods!

Then the wind began to moan. The leaves began to tremble.

It was happening again.

"We're leaving!" cried Annie. "Get down!"

The wind moaned louder. The leaves shook harder.

And the tree house started to spin. It spun faster and faster!

Jack squeezed his eyes shut.

Then everything was still.

Absolutely still.

Jack opened his eyes. He shivered. The air was damp and cool.

The sound of a horse's whinny came again from below.

"Neeee-hhhh!"

"I think we're here," whispered Annie. She was still holding the castle book.

Jack peeked out the window.

A huge castle loomed out of the fog.

He looked around. The tree house was in a different oak tree. And down below, the knight on the black horse was riding by.

"We can't stay here," said Jack. "We have to go home and make a plan first." He picked up the book about Pennsylvania. He opened it to the page with the red silk bookmark. He pointed to the photograph of the Frog Creek woods. "I wish—"

"No!" said Annie. She yanked the book away from him. "Let's stay! I want to visit the castle!"

"You're nuts. We have to examine the situation," said Jack. "From home."

"Let's examine it here!" said Annie.

"Come on." He held out his hand. "Give it."

Annie gave Jack the book. "Okay. You can

go home. I'm staying," she said. She clipped the flashlight to her belt.

"Wait!" said Jack.

"I'm going to take a peek. A teeny peek," she said. And she scooted down the ladder.

Jack groaned. Okay, she had won. He couldn't leave without her. Besides, he sort of wanted to take a peek himself.

He put down the book about Pennsylvania.

He dropped the castle book into his pack. He stepped onto the ladder. And headed down into the cool, misty air.

3

Across the Bridge

Annie was under the tree, looking across the foggy ground.

"The knight's riding toward that bridge, I think," said Annie. "The bridge goes to the castle."

"Wait. I'll look it up," said Jack. "Give me the flashlight!"

He took the flashlight from her and pulled the castle book out of his pack. He opened it to the page with the leather bookmark.

He read the words under the picture of the knight:

> This is a knight arriving for a castle
> feast. Knights wore armor when they
> traveled long and dangerous dis-
> tances. The armor was very heavy.
> A helmet alone could weigh up to
> forty pounds.

Wow. Jack had weighed forty pounds when he was five years old. So it'd be like riding a horse with a five-year-old on your head.

Jack pulled out his notebook. He wanted to take notes, as he'd done on their dinosaur trip.

He wrote:

heavy head

What else?

He turned the pages of the castle book.

He found a picture that showed the whole castle and the buildings around it.

"The knight's crossing the bridge," said Annie. "He's going through the gate. . . . He's gone."

Jack studied the bridge in the picture. He read:

> A drawbridge crossed the moat. The
> moat was filled with water, to help
> protect the castle from enemies.
> Some people believe crocodiles were
> kept in the moat.

Jack wrote in his notebook:

crocodiles in moat?

"Look!" said Annie, peering through the mist. "A windmill! Right over there!"

"Yeah, there's a windmill in here, too," said Jack, pointing at the picture.

"Look at the *real* one, Jack," said Annie. "Not the one in the book."

A piercing shriek split the air.

"Yikes," said Annie. "It sounded like it came from that little house over there!" She pointed through the fog.

"There's a little house *here*," said Jack, studying the picture. He turned the page and read:

> The hawk house was in the inner ward of the castle. Hawks were trained to hunt other birds and small animals.

Jack wrote in his notebook:

hawks in hawk house

"We must be in the inner ward," said Jack.

"Listen!" whispered Annie. "You hear that? Drums! Horns! They're coming from the castle. Let's go see."

"Wait," said Jack. He turned more pages of the book.

"I want to see what's *really* going on, Jack. Not what's in the book," said Annie.

"But look at this!" said Jack.

He pointed to a picture of a big party. Men were standing by the door, playing drums and horns.

He read:

> **Fanfares were played to announce different dishes in a feast. Feasts were held in the Great Hall.**

"You can look at the book. I'm going to the real feast," said Annie.

"Wait," said Jack, studying the picture. It showed boys his age carrying trays of food. Whole pigs. Pies. Peacocks with all their feathers. *Peacocks?*

Jack wrote:

they eat peacocks?

He held up the book to show Annie. "Look, I think they eat—"

Where was she? Gone. Again.

Jack looked through the fog.

He heard the real drums and the real horns. He saw the real hawk house, the real windmill, the real moat.

He saw Annie dashing across the real drawbridge. Then she vanished through the gate leading to the castle.

4

Into the Castle

"I'm going to kill her," muttered Jack.

He threw his stuff into his pack and moved toward the drawbridge. He hoped no one would see him.

It was getting darker. It must be night.

When he got to the bridge, he started across. The wooden planks creaked under his feet.

He peered over the edge of the bridge. Were there any crocodiles in the moat? He couldn't tell.

"Halt!" someone shouted. A guard on top of the castle wall was looking down.

Jack dashed across the bridge. He ran through the castle gate and into the court-yard.

From inside the castle came the sounds of music, shouting, and laughter.

Jack hurried to a dark corner and crouched down. He shivered as he looked around for Annie.

Torches lit the high wall around the courtyard. The courtyard was nearly empty.

Two boys led horses that clopped over the gray cobblestones.

"Neeee-hhhh!"

Jack turned. It was the knight's black horse!

"Psssst!"

He peered into the darkness.

There was Annie.

She was hiding behind a well in the center of the courtyard. She waved at him.

Jack waved back. He waited till the boys and horses disappeared inside the stable. Then he dashed to the well.

"I'm going to find the music!" whispered Annie. "Are you coming?"

"Okay," Jack said with a sigh.

They tiptoed together across the cobblestones. Then they slipped into the entrance of the castle.

Noise and music came from a bright room in front of them. They stood on one side of the doorway and peeked in.

"The feast in the Great Hall!" whispered Jack. He held his breath as he stared in awe.

A giant fireplace blazed at one end of the noisy room. Antlers and rugs hung on the stone walls. Flowers covered the floor. Boys in short dresses carried huge trays of food.

Dogs were fighting over bones under the tables.

People in bright clothes and funny hats strolled among the crowd. Some played funny-shaped guitars. Some tossed balls in the air. Some balanced swords on their hands.

Men and women dressed in capes and furs sat at long, crowded wooden tables.

"I wonder which one is the knight," said Jack.

"I don't know," whispered Annie. "But they're eating with their fingers."

Suddenly, someone shouted behind them.

Jack whirled around.

A man carrying a tray of pies was standing a few feet away.

"Who art thou?" he asked angrily.

"Jack," squeaked Jack.

"Annie," squeaked Annie.

Then they ran as fast as they could down
a dimly lit hallway.

5

Trapped

"Come on!" cried Annie.

Jack raced behind her.

Were they being followed?

"Here! Quick!" Annie dashed toward a door off the hallway. She pushed the door open. The two of them stumbled into a dark, cold room. The door creaked shut behind them.

"Give me the flashlight," said Annie. Jack handed it to her, and she switched it on.

Yikes! A row of knights right in front of them!

Annie flicked off the light.

Silence.

"They aren't moving," Jack whispered.

Annie turned the light back on.

"They're just suits," Jack said.

"Without heads," said Annie.

"Let me have the flashlight a second," said Jack. "So I can look in the book."

Annie handed him the flashlight. He pulled out the castle book. He flipped through the pages until he found what he was looking for.

Jack put the book away. "It's called the armory," he said. "It's where armor and weapons are stored."

He shined the flashlight around the room.

"Oh, man," whispered Jack.

The light fell on shiny breastplates, leg plates, arm plates. On shelves filled with helmets and weapons. On shields, spears, swords, crossbows, clubs, battle-axes.

There was a noise in the hall. Voices!

"Let's hide!" said Annie.

"Wait," said Jack. "I got to check on something first."

"Hurry," said Annie.

"It'll take just a second," said Jack. "Hold this." He handed Annie the flashlight.

He tried to lift a helmet from a shelf. It was too heavy.

He bent over and dragged the helmet over his head. The visor slammed shut.

Oh, forget it. It was *worse* than having a five-year-old on your head. More like having a ten-year-old on your head.

Not only could Jack not lift his head, he couldn't see anything, either.

"Jack!" Annie's voice sounded far away.

"The voices are getting closer!"

"Turn off the flashlight!" Jack's voice echoed inside the metal chamber.

He struggled to get the helmet off.

Suddenly he lost his balance and went crashing into other pieces of armor.

The metal plates and weapons clattered to the floor.

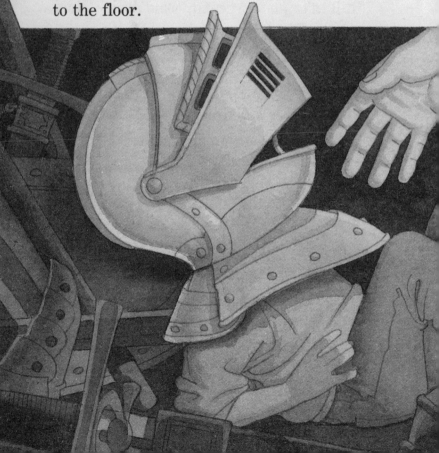

Jack lay on the floor in the dark.

He tried to get up. But his head was too heavy.

He heard deep voices.

Someone grabbed him by the arm. The next thing he knew, his helmet was yanked off. He was staring into the blazing light of a fiery torch.

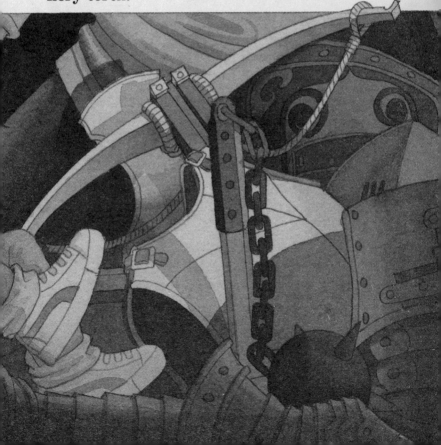

6

Ta-da!

In the torchlight, Jack saw three huge men standing over him.

One with very squinty eyes held the torch. One with a very red face held Jack. And one with a very long mustache held on to Annie.

Annie was kicking and yelling.

"Stop!" said the one with the very long mustache.

"Who art thou?" said the one with the very red face.

"Spies? Foreigners? Egyptians? Romans? Persians?" said the squinty-eyed one.

"No, you dummies!" said Annie.

"Oh, brother," Jack muttered.

"Arrest them!" said Red-face.

"The dungeon!" said Squinty-eyes.

The guards marched Jack and Annie out of the armory. Jack looked back frantically. Where was his backpack?

"Go!" said a guard, giving him a push.

Jack went.

Down they marched, down the long, dark hallway. Squinty, Annie, Mustache, Jack, and Red.

Down a narrow, winding staircase.

Jack heard Annie shouting at the guards. "Dummies! Meanies! We didn't do anything!"

The guards laughed. They didn't take her seriously at all.

At the bottom of the stairs was a big iron door with a bar across it.

Squinty pushed the bar off the door. Then he shoved at the door. It creaked open.

Jack and Annie were pushed into a cold, clammy room.

The fiery torch lit the dungeon. There were chains hanging from the filthy walls. Water dripped from the ceiling, making puddles on the stone floor. It was the creepiest place Jack had ever seen.

"We'll keep them here till the feast is done. Then turn them over to the Duke," said Squinty. "He knows how to take care of thieves."

"There will be a hanging tomorrow," said Mustache.

"If the rats don't get them first," said Red.

They all laughed.

Jack saw that Annie had his backpack. She was quietly unzipping it.

"Come on, let's chain the two of 'em," said Squinty.

The guards started toward them. Annie whipped her flashlight out of the pack.

"Ta-da!" she yelled.

The guards froze. They stared at the shiny flashlight in her hand.

Annie switched the light on. The guards gasped in fear. They jumped back against the wall.

Squinty dropped the torch. It fell into a dirty puddle on the floor, sputtered, and went out.

"My magic wand!" Annie said, waving the flashlight. "Get down. Or I'll wipe you out!"

Jack's mouth dropped open.

Annie fiercely pointed her light at one, then the other. Each howled and covered his face.

"Down! All of you! Get down!" shouted Annie.

One by one, the guards lay down on the wet floor.

Jack couldn't believe it.

"Come on," Annie said to him. "Let's go."

Jack looked at the open doorway. He looked at the guards quaking on the ground.

"Hurry!" said Annie.

In one quick leap, Jack followed her out of the terrible dungeon.

7

A Secret Passage

Annie and Jack raced back up the winding
stairs and down the long hallway.

They hadn't gone far when they heard
shouting behind them.

Dogs barked in the distance.

"They're coming!" Annie cried.

"In here!" said Jack. He shoved open a
door off the hallway and pulled Annie into a
dark room.

Jack pushed the door shut. Then Annie
shined her flashlight around the room. There
were rows of sacks and wooden barrels.

"I'd better look in the book," said Jack. "Give it to me!"

Annie gave him the flashlight and his backpack. He pulled out the book and started tearing through it.

"Shhh!" said Annie. "Someone's coming."

Jack and Annie jumped behind the door as it creaked open.

Jack held his breath. A light from a torch danced wildly over the sacks and barrels.

The light disappeared. The door slammed shut.

"Oh, man," whispered Jack. "We have to hurry. They might come back."

His hands were trembling as he flipped through the pages of the castle book.

"Here's a map of the castle," he said. "Look, this must be the room we're in. It's a storeroom." Jack studied the room in the book.

"These are sacks of flour and barrels of wine."

"Who cares? We have to go!" said Annie. "Before they come back!"

"No. Look," said Jack. He pointed at the map. "Here's a trapdoor."

He read aloud:

> This door leads from the storeroom
> through a secret passage to a
> precipice over the moat.

"What's a precipice?" said Annie.

"I don't know. We'll find out," said Jack. "But first we have to find the door."

Jack looked at the picture carefully. Then he shined the flashlight around the room.

The floor of the room was made up of stones. The trapdoor in the picture was five stones away from the door to the hall.

Jack shined the light on the floor and

counted the stones. "One, two, three, four, five."

He stamped on the fifth stone. It was loose!

He put the flashlight on the floor. He worked his fingers under the thin sheet of stone and tried to lift it.

"Help," Jack said.

Annie came over and helped him lift the stone square out of its place. Underneath was a small wooden door.

Jack and Annie tugged on the rope handle of the door. The door fell open with a thunk.

Jack picked up the flashlight and shined it on the hole.

"There's a little ladder," he said. "Let's go!"

He clipped on the flashlight and felt his way down the small ladder. Annie followed.

When they both reached the bottom of the ladder, Jack shined the light around them.

There was a tunnel!

He crouched down and began moving through the damp, creepy tunnel. The flashlight barely lit the stone walls.

He shook the light. Were the batteries running down?

"I think our light's dying!" he said to Annie.

"Hurry!" she called from behind.

Jack went faster. His back hurt from crouching.

The light got dimmer and dimmer.

He was desperate to get out of the castle before the batteries died completely.

Soon he reached another small wooden door. The door at the end of the tunnel!

Jack unlatched the door and pushed it open.

He poked his head outside.

He couldn't see anything in the misty darkness.

The air felt good. Cool and fresh. He took a deep breath.

"Where are we?" whispered Annie behind him. "What do you see?"

"Nothing. But I think we've come to the outside of the castle," said Jack. "I'll find out."

Jack put the flashlight in his pack. He put the pack on his back. He stuck his hand out the door. He couldn't feel the ground. Just air.

"I'm going to have to go feet first," he said.

Jack turned around in the small tunnel. He lay down on his stomach. He stuck one

leg out the door. Then the other.

Jack inched down, bit by bit. Until he was hanging out the door, clinging to the ledge.

"This must be the precipice!" he called to Annie. "Pull me up!"

Annie reached for Jack's hands. "I can't hold you!" she said.

Jack felt his fingers slipping. Then down he fell.

Down through the darkness.

SPLASH!

8

The Knight

Water filled Jack's nose and covered his head.
His glasses fell off. He grabbed them just in
time. He coughed and flailed his arms.

"Jack!" Annie was calling from above.

"I'm in . . . the moat!" said Jack, gasping
for air. He tried to tread water and put his
glasses back on. With his backpack, his shoes,
and his heavy clothes, he could hardly stay
afloat.

SPLASH!

"Hi! I'm here!" Annie sputtered.

Jack could hear her nearby. But he couldn't see her.

"Which way's land?" Annie asked.

"I don't know! Just swim!"

Jack dog-paddled through the cold black water.

He heard Annie swimming, too. At first it seemed as if she was swimming in front of him. But then he heard a splash behind him.

"Annie?" he called.

"What?" Her voice came from in front. Not behind.

Another splash. *Behind*.

Jack's heart almost stopped. Crocodiles? He couldn't see anything through his water-streaked glasses.

"Annie!" he whispered.

"What?"

"Swim faster!"

"But I'm here! I'm over here! Near the edge!" she whispered.

Jack swam through the dark toward her voice. He imagined a crocodile slithering after him.

Another splash! Not far away!

Jack's hand touched a wet, live thing.

"Ahhhh!" he cried.

"It's me! Take my hand!" said Annie.

Jack grabbed her hand. She pulled him to the edge of the moat. They crawled over an embankment onto the wet grass.

Safe!

Another splash came from the moat waters.

"Oh, man," Jack said.

He was shivering all over. His teeth were

chattering. He shook the water off his glasses and put them back on.

It was so misty he couldn't see the castle. He couldn't even see the moat, much less a crocodile.

"We . . . we made it," said Annie. Her teeth were chattering, too.

"I know," said Jack. "But where are we?" He peered at the foggy darkness.

Where was the drawbridge? The windmill? The hawk house? The grove of trees? The tree house?

Everything had been swallowed up by the thick, soupy darkness.

Jack reached into his wet backpack and pulled out the flashlight. He pushed the switch. No more light.

They were trapped. Not in a dungeon. But in the still, cold darkness.

"Neeee-hhhh!"

A horse's whinny.

Just then the clouds parted. A full moon was shining in the sky. A pool of light spread through the mist.

Then Jack and Annie saw him just a few feet away. The knight.

He sat on the black horse. His armor shone in the moonlight. A visor hid his face. But he seemed to be staring straight at Jack and Annie.

9

Under the Moon

Jack froze.

"It's him," Annie whispered.

The knight held out his gloved hand.

"Come on, Jack," Annie said.

"Where are you going?" said Jack.

"He wants to help us," said Annie.

"How do you know?"

"I can just tell," said Annie.

Annie stepped toward the horse. The knight dismounted.

The knight picked Annie up and put her on the back of his horse.

"Come on, Jack," she called.

Jack moved slowly toward the knight. It was like a dream.

The knight picked him up, too. He placed Jack on the horse, behind Annie.

The knight got on behind them. He slapped the reins.

The black horse cantered beside the moonlit water of the moat.

Jack rocked back and forth in the saddle. The wind blew his hair. He felt very brave and very powerful.

He felt as if he could ride forever on this horse, with this mysterious knight. Over the ocean. Over the world. Over the moon.

A hawk shrieked in the darkness.

"There's the tree house," said Annie. She pointed toward a grove of trees.

The knight steered the horse toward the trees.

"See. There it is," Annie said, pointing to the ladder.

The knight brought his horse to a stop. He dismounted and helped Annie down.

"Thank you, sir," she said. And she bowed.

Then Jack. "Thank you," he said. And he bowed also.

The knight got back on his horse. He raised his gloved hand. Then he slapped the reins and rode off through the mist.

Annie started up the tall ladder, and Jack followed. They climbed into the dark tree house and looked out the window.

The knight was riding toward the outer wall. They saw him go through the outer gate.

Clouds started to cover the moon again.

For a brief moment, Jack thought he saw the knight's armor gleaming on the top of a hill beyond the castle.

The clouds covered the moon completely. And a black mist swallowed the land.

"He's gone," whispered Annie.

Jack shivered in his wet clothes as he kept staring at the blackness.

"I'm cold," said Annie. "Where's the Pennsylvania book?"

Jack heard Annie fumble in the darkness. He kept looking out the window.

"I think this is it," said Annie. "I feel a silk bookmark."

Jack was only half-listening. He was hoping to see the knight's armor gleam again in the distance.

"Okay. I'm going to use this," said Annie. "Because I think it's the right one.

Here goes. Okay. I'm pointing. I'm going to wish. I wish we could go to Frog Creek!"

Jack heard the wind begin to blow. Softly at first.

"I hope I pointed to the right picture in the right book," said Annie.

"What?" Jack looked back at her. "Right picture? Right book?"

The tree house began to rock. The wind got louder and louder.

"I hope it wasn't the dinosaur book!" said Annie.

"Stop!" Jack shouted at the tree house.

Too late.

The tree house started to spin. It was spinning and spinning!

The wind was screaming.

Then suddenly there was silence.

Absolute silence.

10

One Mystery Solved

The air was warm.

It was dawn. Far away a dog barked.

"I think that's Henry barking!" Annie said. "We *did* come home."

They both looked out the tree house window.

"That was close," said Jack.

In the distance, streetlights lit their street. There was a light on in their upstairs window.

"Uh-oh," said Annie. "I think Mom and Dad are up. Hurry!"

"Wait." In a daze, Jack unzipped his backpack. He pulled out the castle book. It was quite wet. But Jack placed it back with all the other books.

"Come on! Hurry!" said Annie, scooting out of the tree house.

Jack followed her down the ladder.

They reached the ground and took off between the gray-black trees.

They left the woods and ran down their deserted street.

They got to their yard and crept across the lawn. Right up to the back door.

Jack and Annie slipped inside the house.

"They're not downstairs yet," whispered Annie.

"Shhh," said Jack.

He led the way up the stairs and down the hall. No sign of his mom or dad. But he could hear water running in the bathroom.

Their house was so different from the dark, cold castle. So safe and cozy and friendly.

Annie stopped at her bedroom door. She gave Jack a smile, then disappeared inside her room.

Jack hurried into his room. He took off his damp clothes and pulled on his dry, soft pajamas.

He sat down on his bed and unzipped his backpack. He took out his wet notebook. He felt around for the pencil, but his hand touched something else.

Jack pulled the blue leather bookmark out of his pack. It must have fallen out of the castle book.

Jack held the bookmark close to his lamp and studied it. The leather was smooth and worn. It seemed ancient.

For the first time Jack noticed a letter on the bookmark. A fancy M.

Jack opened the drawer next to his bed. He took out the gold medallion.

He looked at the letter on it. It was the same M.

Now this was an amazing new fact.

Jack took a deep breath. One mystery solved.

The person who had dropped the gold medallion in the time of the dinosaurs was the same person who owned all the books in the tree house.

Who *was* this person?

Jack placed the bookmark next to the medallion. He closed the drawer.

He picked up his pencil. He turned to the

least wet page in his notebook. And he started to write down this new fact.

the same

But before he could draw the M, his eyes closed.

He dreamed they were with the knight again. All three of them riding the black horse through the cool, dark night. Beyond the outer wall of the castle. And up over a moonlit hill.

Into the mist.

Mummies
in the Morning

For Patrick Robbins,
who loves ancient Egypt

Contents

1

Meow!

"It's still here," said Jack.

"It looks empty," said Annie.

Jack and his seven-year-old sister gazed up at a very tall oak tree. At the top of the tree was a tree house.

Late-morning sunlight lit the woods. It was almost time for lunch.

"Shhh!" said Jack. "What was that noise?"

"What noise?"

"I heard a noise," Jack said. He looked around. "It sounded like someone coughing."

"I didn't hear anything," said Annie. "Come on. Let's go up."

She grabbed onto the rope ladder and started climbing.

Jack tiptoed over to a clump of bushes. He pushed aside a small branch.

"Hello?" he said. "Anybody there?"

There was no answer.

"Come on!" Annie called down. "The tree house looks the same as it did yesterday."

Jack still felt that someone was nearby. Could it be the person who'd put all the books in the tree house?

"Ja-ack!"

Jack gazed over the top of the bushes.

Was the mysterious person watching him now? The person whose name began with M?

Maybe M wanted the gold medallion back. The one Jack had found on their dinosaur adventure. Maybe M wanted the leather bookmark back. The one from the castle book.

There was an M on the medallion. And an M on the bookmark. But what did M stand for?

"Tomorrow I'll bring everything back," Jack said loudly.

A breeze swept through the woods. The leaves rattled.

"Come on!" called Annie.

Jack went back to the big oak tree. He grabbed onto the rope ladder and climbed up.

At the top he crawled through a hole in the wooden floor. He tossed down his backpack and pushed his glasses into place.

"Hmmm. Which book is it going to be today?" said Annie.

She was looking at the books scattered around the tree house.

Annie picked up the book about castles.

"Hey, this isn't wet anymore," she said.

"Let me see."

Jack took the book from her. He was amazed. It looked fine. Yesterday it had gotten soaked in a castle moat.

The castle book had taken Jack and Annie back to the time of knights.

Jack silently thanked the mysterious knight who had rescued them.

"Watch out!" warned Annie.

She waved a dinosaur book in Jack's face.

"Put that away," said Jack.

The day before yesterday the dinosaur book had taken them to the time of dinosaurs.

Jack silently thanked the Pteranodon who had saved him from a Tyrannosaurus rex.

Annie put the dinosaur book back with the other books. Then she gasped.

"Wow," she whispered. "Look at *this*."

She held up a book about ancient Egypt.

Jack caught his breath. He took the book from her. A green silk bookmark stuck out of it.

Jack turned to the page with the bookmark. There was a picture of a pyramid.

Going toward the pyramid was a long parade. Four huge cows with horns were pulling a sled. On the sled was a long gold box. Many Egyptians were walking behind the sled. At the end of the parade was a sleek black cat.

"Let's go there," whispered Annie. "Now."

"Wait," said Jack. He wanted to study the book a bit more.

"Pyramids, Jack," said Annie. "You love pyramids."

It was true. Pyramids *were* high on his list

of favorite things. After knights. But before dinosaurs. *Way* before dinosaurs.

He didn't have to worry about being eaten by a pyramid.

"Okay," he said. "But hold the Pennsylvania book. In case we want to come right back here."

Annie found the book with the picture of their hometown in it. Frog Creek, Pennsylvania.

Then Jack pointed to the pyramid picture in the Egypt book. He cleared his throat and said, "I wish we could go to this place."

"Meow!"

"What was *that?*" Jack looked out the tree house window.

A black cat was perched on a branch. Right outside the window. The cat was staring at Jack and Annie.

It was the strangest cat Jack had ever seen. He was very sleek and dark. With bright yellow eyes. And a wide gold collar.

"It's the cat in the Egypt book," whispered Annie.

Just then the wind started to blow. The leaves began to shake.

"Here we go!" cried Annie.

The wind whistled louder. The leaves shook harder.

Jack closed his eyes as the tree house started to spin.

It spun faster and faster! And faster!

Suddenly everything was still.

Absolutely still.

Not a sound. Not a whisper.

Jack opened his eyes.

Hot bright sunlight nearly blinded him.

"Me-ow!"

2

Oh, Man. Mummies!

Jack and Annie looked out the window.

The tree house was perched on the top of a palm tree. The tree stood with other palm trees. A patch of green surrounded by a sandy desert.

"Meow!"

Jack and Annie looked down.

The black cat was sitting at the base of the tree. His yellow eyes were staring up at Jack and Annie.

"Hi!" Annie shouted.

"Shhh," said Jack. "Someone might hear you."

"In the middle of the desert?" said Annie.

The black cat stood and began walking around the tree.

"Come back!" Annie called. She leaned out the window to see where the cat was going.

"Oh, wow!" she said. "Look, Jack."

Jack leaned forward and looked down.

The cat was running away from the palm trees. Toward a giant pyramid in the desert.

A parade was going toward the pyramid. The same parade as in the Egypt book.

"It's the picture from the book!" said Jack.

"What are those people doing?" asked Annie.

Jack looked down at the Egypt book. He read the words under the picture:

> When a royal person died, a grand funeral procession took place. Family, servants, and mourners followed the coffin. The coffin was called a sarcophagus. It was pulled on a sled by four oxen.

"It's an Egyptian funeral," said Jack. "The box is called a sar...sar...sar...oh, forget it."

He looked out the window again.

Oxen, sled, Egyptians, black cat. All were moving in a slow, dreamy way.

"I'd better make some notes about this," said Jack.

He reached into his backpack and pulled out his notebook. Jack always kept notes.

"Wait," said Jack. And he wrote:

Coffin called sarcophagus

"We'd better hurry," said Annie, "if we want to see the mummy."

She started down the rope ladder.

Jack looked up from his notebook.

"Mummy?" he said.

"There's probably a mummy in that gold box," Annie called up. "We're in ancient Egypt. Remember?"

Jack loved mummies. He put down his pencil.

"Good-bye, Jack!" called Annie.

"Wait!" Jack called.

"Mummies!" Annie shouted.

"Oh, man," said Jack weakly. "Mummies!" She sure knew how to get to him.

Jack shoved his notebook and the Egypt book into his pack. Then he started down the ladder.

When he got to the ground, he and Annie took off across the sand.

But as they ran a strange thing happened.

The closer they got to the parade, the harder it was to see it.

Then suddenly it was gone. The strange parade had disappeared. Vanished.

But the great stone pyramid was still there. Towering above them.

Panting, Jack looked around.

What had happened? Where were the people? The oxen? The gold box? The cat?

"They're gone," said Annie.

"Where did they go?" said Jack.

"Maybe they were ghosts," said Annie.

"Don't be silly. There's no such thing as ghosts," said Jack. "It must have been a mirage."

"A what?"

"Mirage. It happens in the desert all the time," said Jack. "It looks like something's there. But it just turns out to be the sunlight reflecting through heat."

"How could sunlight look like people, a mummy box, and a bunch of cows?" said Annie.

Jack frowned.

"Ghosts," she said.

"No way," said Jack.

"Look!" Annie pointed at the pyramid. Near the base was the sleek black cat.

He was standing alone. He was staring at Jack and Annie.

"*He*'s no mirage," said Annie.

The cat started to slink away. He walked along the base of the pyramid and slid around a corner.

"Where's he going?" said Jack.

"Let's find out," said Annie.

They dashed around the corner—just in time to see the cat disappear through a hole in the pyramid.

3

It's Alive!

"Where did he go?" said Jack.

He and Annie peeked through the hole.

They saw a long hallway. Burning torches lit the walls. Dark shadows loomed.

"Let's go in," said Annie.

"Wait," said Jack.

He pulled out the Egypt book and turned to the section on pyramids.

He read the caption aloud:

> Pyramids were sometimes called
> Houses of the Dead. They were
> nearly all solid stone, except for
> the burial chambers deep inside.

"Wow. Let's go there. To the burial chambers," said Annie. "I bet a mummy's there."

Jack took a deep breath.

Then he stepped out of the hot, bright sunlight into the cool, dark pyramid.

The hallway was silent.

Floor, ceiling, walls—everything was stone.

The floor slanted up from where they stood.

"We have to go farther inside," said Annie.

"Right," said Jack. "But stay close behind me. Don't talk. Don't—"

"Go! Just go!" said Annie. She gave him a little push.

Jack started up the slanting floor of the hallway.

Where was the cat?

The hallway went on and on.

"Wait," said Jack. "I want to look at the book."

He opened the Egypt book again. He held it below a torch on the wall. The book showed a picture of the inside of the pyramid.

"The burial chamber is in the middle of the pyramid. See?" Jack said. He pointed to the picture. "It seems to be straight ahead."

Jack tucked the book under his arm. Then they headed deeper into the pyramid.

Soon the floor became flat. The air felt different. Musty and stale.

Jack opened the book again. "I think we're almost at the burial chamber. See the picture? The hallway slants up. Then it gets flat. Then you come to the chamber. See, look—"

"Eee-eee!" A strange cry shot through the pyramid.

Jack dropped the Egypt book.

Out of the shadows flew a white figure.

It swooshed toward them!

A mummy!

"It's alive!" Annie shouted.

4

Back from the Dead

Jack pulled Annie down.

The white figure moved swiftly past them. Then disappeared into the shadows.

"A mummy," said Annie. "Back from the dead!"

"F-forget it," stammered Jack. "Mummies aren't alive." He picked up the Egypt book.

"What's this?" said Annie. She lifted something from the floor. "Look. The mummy dropped this thing."

It was a gold stick. About a foot long. A dog's head was carved on one end.

"It looks like a scepter," said Jack.

"What's that?" asked Annie.

"It's a thing kings and queens carry," said Jack. "It means they have power over the people."

"Come back, mummy!" Annie called. "We found your scepter. Come back! We want to help you!"

"Shush!" said Jack. "Are you nuts?"

"But the mummy—"

"That was no mummy," said Jack. "It was a person. A real person."

"What kind of person would be inside a pyramid?" asked Annie.

"I don't know," said Jack. "Maybe the book can help us."

He flipped through the book. At last he found a picture of a person in a pyramid. He read:

> Tomb robbers often carried off the
> treasure buried with mummies.
> False passages were sometimes
> built to stop the robbers.

Jack closed the book.

"No live mummy," he said. "Just a tomb robber."

"Yikes. A tomb robber?" said Annie.

"Yeah, a robber who steals stuff from tombs."

"But what if the robber comes back," said Annie. "We'd better leave."

"Right," said Jack. "But first I want to write something down."

He put the Egypt book into his pack. He pulled out his notebook and pencil.

He started writing in his notebook:

tomb robber

"Jack—" said Annie.

"Just a second," said Jack. He kept writing:

tomb robber tried to steal

"Jack! Look!" said Annie.

Jack felt a whoosh of cold air. He looked up. A wave of terror went through him.

Another figure was moving slowly toward them.

It wasn't a tomb robber.

No. It was a lady. A beautiful Egyptian lady.

She wore flowers in her black hair. Her long white dress had many tiny pleats. Her gold jewelry glittered.

"Here, Jack," Annie whispered. "Give her this." She handed him the gold scepter.

The lady stopped in front of them.

Jack held out the scepter. His hand was trembling.

He gasped. The scepter passed right through the lady's hand.

She was made of air.

5

The Ghost-Queen

"A ghost," Annie whispered.

But Jack could only stare in horror.

The ghost began to speak. She spoke in a hollow, echoing voice.

"I am Hutepi," she said. "Queen of the Nile. Is it true that you have come to help me?"

"Yes," said Annie.

Jack still couldn't speak.

"For a thousand years," said the ghost-queen, "I have waited for help."

Jack's heart was pounding so hard he

thought he might faint.

"Someone must find my Book of the Dead," she said. "I need it to go on to the Next Life."

"Why do you need the Book of the Dead?" asked Annie. She didn't sound scared at all.

"It will tell me the magic spells I need to get through the Underworld," said the ghost-queen.

"The Underworld?" said Annie.

"Before I journey on to the Next Life, I must pass through the horrors of the Underworld."

"What kinds of horrors?" Annie asked.

"Poisonous snakes," said the ghost-queen. "Lakes of fire. Monsters. Demons."

"Oh." Annie stepped closer to Jack.

"My brother hid the Book of the Dead. So tomb robbers would not steal it," said the ghost-queen. "Then he carved this secret message on the wall, telling me how to find it."

She pointed to the wall.

Jack was still in shock. He couldn't move.

"Where?" asked Annie. "Here?" She squinted at the wall. "What do these tiny pictures mean?"

The ghost-queen smiled sadly. "Alas, my brother forgot my strange problem. I cannot

see clearly that which is close to my eyes. I have not been able to read his message for a thousand years."

"Oh, that's not a strange problem," said Annie. "Jack can't see anything either. That's why he wears glasses."

The ghost-queen stared in wonder at Jack.

"Jack, lend her your glasses," said Annie.

Jack took his glasses off his nose. He held them out to the ghost-queen.

She backed away from him. "I fear I cannot wear your glasses, Jack," she said. "I am made of air."

"Oh. I forgot," said Annie.

"But perhaps you will describe the hieroglyphs on these walls," said the ghost-queen.

"Hi-row-who?" said Annie.

"Hieroglyphs!" said Jack, finally finding his voice. "It's the ancient Egyptian way of writing. It's like writing with pictures."

The ghost-queen smiled at him. "Thank you, Jack," she said.

Jack smiled back at her. He put his glasses on. Then he stepped toward the wall and took a good long look.

"Oh, man," he whispered.

6

The Writing on the Wall

Jack and Annie squinted at the pyramid wall.

A series of tiny pictures were carved into the stone.

"There are four pictures here," Jack told the ghost-queen.

"Describe them to me, Jack. One at a time, please," she said.

Jack studied the first picture.

"Okay," he said. "The first one is like this."
He made a zigzag in the air with his finger.

"Like stairs?" asked the ghost-queen.

"Yes, stairs!" said Jack. "Just like stairs."

She nodded.

Easy enough.

Jack studied the second picture.

"The second one has a long box on the bottom," he said. He drew it in the air.

The ghost-queen looked puzzled.

"With three things on top. Like this," said Annie. She drew squiggly lines in the air.

The ghost-queen still seemed puzzled.

"Like a hat," said Jack.

"Hat?" said the ghost-queen.

"No. More like a boat," said Annie.

"Boat?" said the ghost-queen. She got excited. "Boat?"

Jack took another look at the wall.

"Yes. It could be a boat," he said.

The ghost-queen looked very happy. She smiled.

"Yes. Of course," she said.

Jack and Annie studied the next picture.

"The third one is like a thing that holds flowers," said Annie.

"Or a thing that holds water," said Jack.

"Like a jug?" asked the ghost-queen.

"Exactly," said Jack.

"Yes. A jug," said Annie.

Jack and Annie studied the last picture.

"And the last one looks like a pole that droops," said Annie.

"Like a curved stick," said Jack. "But one side is shorter than the other."

The ghost-queen looked puzzled.

"Wait," said Jack. "I'll draw it in my notebook. Big! So you can see it."

Jack put down the scepter and got out his pencil. He drew the hieroglyph.

"A folded cloth," said the ghost-queen.

"Well, not really," said Jack. He studied his drawing.

"But that is the hieroglyph for a folded cloth," said the ghost-queen.

"Well, okay," said Jack.

He looked at the fourth hieroglyph again. He still couldn't see the folded cloth. Unless it was like a towel hanging over a bathroom rod.

"So that's all of them," said Annie. She pointed at each picture. "Stairs. Boat. Jug. Folded cloth."

Jack wrote the words in his notebook.

stairs = ⌐┌┘   Jug = ▢

boat = ⌐Ⱶ⌐   Cloth = ⌐

"So what does the message mean?" he asked the ghost-queen.

"Come," she said. She held out her hand. "Come to my burial chambers."

And she floated away.

7

The Scroll

Jack put the scepter and his notebook and pencil into his pack.

He and Annie followed the ghost-queen. Deeper into the pyramid. Until they came to some stairs.

"The STAIRS!" said Jack and Annie.

The ghost-queen floated up the stairs.

Jack and Annie followed.

The ghost-queen floated right through a wooden door.

Jack and Annie pushed on the door. It opened slowly.

They stepped into a cold, drafty room.

The ghost-queen was nowhere in sight.

Dim torchlight lit the huge room. It had a very high ceiling. On one side was a pile of tables, chairs, and musical instruments.

On the other side of the room was a small wooden boat.

"The BOAT!" said Jack.

"What's it doing inside Queen Hutepi's pyramid?" asked Annie.

"Maybe it's supposed to carry her to the Next Life," said Jack.

He and Annie went over to the boat. They looked inside it.

The boat was filled with many things. Gold plates. Painted cups. Jeweled goblets. Woven baskets. Jewelry with blue stones. Small wooden statues.

"Look!" said Jack.

He reached into the boat and lifted out a clay jug.

"The JUG!" said Annie.

Jack looked inside the jug.

"Something's in here," he said.

"What is it?" asked Annie.

Jack felt down inside the jug.

"It feels like a big napkin," he said.

"The FOLDED CLOTH!" said Annie.

Jack reached into the jug and pulled out the folded cloth. It was wrapped around an ancient-looking scroll.

Jack slowly unrolled the scroll.

It was covered with wonderful hieroglyphs.

"The Book of the Dead!" whispered Annie. "We found it. We found her book."

"Oh, man." Jack traced his finger over the scroll. It felt like very old paper.

"Queen Hutepi!" called Annie. "We have it! We found your Book of the Dead!"

Silence.

"Queen Hutepi!"

Then another door on the other side of the chamber creaked open.

"In there," said Annie. "Maybe she's in there."

Jack's heart was pounding. Cold air was coming through the open doorway.

"Come on," said Annie.

"Wait—"

"No," said Annie. "She's waited a thousand years for her book. Don't make her wait anymore."

Jack put the ancient scroll into his backpack. Then he and Annie slowly started to cross the drafty room.

They came to the open door. Annie went through first.

"Hurry, Jack!" she said.

Jack stepped into the other room.

It was nearly bare. Except for a long gold

box. The box was open. The cover was on the floor.

"Queen Hutepi?" called Annie.

Silence.

"We found it," said Annie. "Your Book of the Dead."

There was still no sign of the ghost-queen.

The gold box glowed.

Jack could barely breathe. "Let's leave the scroll on the floor. And go," he said.

"No. I think we should leave it in there," said Annie. She pointed to the gold box.

"No," said Jack.

"Don't be afraid," said Annie. "Come on."

Annie took Jack by the arm. They walked together. Across the room. To the glowing gold box.

They stopped in front of the box. And they peered inside.

8

The Mummy

A real mummy.

Bandages were still wrapped around the bald skull. But most of the bandages had come off the face.

It was Hutepi. Queen of the Nile.

Her broken teeth were showing. Her little wrinkled ears. Her squashed nose. Her withered flesh. Her hollow eye sockets.

Plus the rotting bandages on her body were coming off. You could see bones.

"Oh, gross!" cried Annie. "Let's go!"

"No," said Jack. "It's interesting."

"Forget it!" said Annie. She started out of the room.

"Wait, Annie."

"Come on, Jack. Hurry!" cried Annie. She was standing by the door.

Jack pulled out the Egypt book and flipped to a picture of a mummy. He read aloud:

> Ancient Egyptians tried to protect the body so it would last forever. First it was dried out with salt.

"Ugh, stop!" said Annie.

"Listen," said Jack. He kept reading:

> Next it was covered with oil. Then it was wrapped tightly in bandages. The brain was removed by—

"Yuck! Stop!" cried Annie. "Good-bye!" She dashed out of the room.

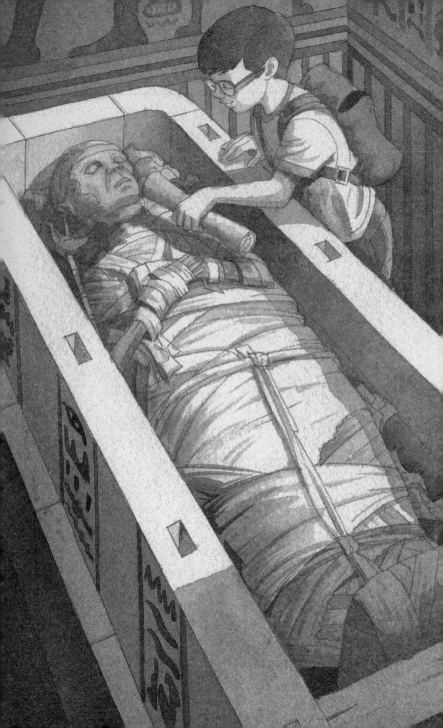

"Annie!" called Jack. "We have to give her the Book of the Dead!"

But Annie was gone.

Jack reached into his pack. He pulled out the scroll and the scepter. He put them next to the mummy's skull.

Was it just his imagination? Or did a deep sigh seem to shudder throughout the room? Did the mummy's face grow calmer?

Jack held his breath as he backed away. Out of the mummy room. Out of the boat room. Down the stairs.

At the bottom of the stairs, he heaved his own sigh. A sigh of relief.

He looked down the hallway. It was empty.

"Hey! Where are you?" he said.

No answer.

Where in the world was Annie?

Jack started down the hallway.

"Annie!" he called.

Had she run out of the pyramid? Was she already outside?

"Annie!"

"Help, Jack!" came a cry. The voice sounded far away.

It was Annie! Where was she?

"Help, Jack!"

"Annie!"

Jack started to run. Along the shadowy hallway.

"Help, Jack!" Her cry seemed fainter.

Jack stopped.

He was running *away* from her voice.

"Annie!" he called. He went back toward the burial chambers.

"Jack!"

There! Her voice was louder.

"Jack!"

Even louder!

Jack climbed the stairs. He went back into the boat room.

He looked around the room. At the furniture. The musical instruments. The boat.

Then he saw it. Another door! Right next to the door he had just come through.

The other door was open.

Jack dashed through it. He found himself at the top of some stairs.

They were just like the stairs in the other hallway.

He went down into the hallway. It was lit by torches on the wall.

It was just like the other hallway.

"Annie!" he called.

"Jack!"

"Annie!"

"Jack!"

She was running through the hallway toward him.

She crashed into him.

"I was lost!" she cried.

"I think this is one of those false passages. Built to fool the tomb robbers," said Jack.

"A false passage?" said Annie, panting.

"Yeah, it looks just like the right hallway," said Jack. "We have to go back into the boat room. And out the right door."

Just then they heard a creaking noise.

Jack and Annie turned around. They looked up the stairs.

Then they watched in horror as the door slowly creaked shut.

A deep sound rumbled in the distance. And all the torches went out.

9

Follow the Leader

It was pitch dark.

"What happened?" asked Annie.

"I don't know. Something weird," said Jack. "We have to get out of here fast. Push against the door."

"Good idea," said Annie in a small voice.

They felt their way through the darkness. To the top of the stairs.

"Don't worry. Everything's going to be okay," said Jack. He was trying to stay calm.

"Of course," said Annie.

They leaned against the wooden door and pushed.

It wouldn't budge.

They pushed harder.

No use.

Jack took a deep breath. It was getting harder to breathe. And harder to stay calm.

"What can we do?" asked Annie.

"Just...just rest a moment," said Jack, panting.

His heart was pounding as he tried to see through the darkness.

"Maybe we should start down the hall," he said. "Maybe we'll eventually come to...to an exit."

He wasn't sure about that. But they had no choice.

"Come on," he said. "Feel the wall."

Jack felt the stone wall as he climbed slowly down the stairs. Annie followed.

Jack started down the dark hallway. It

was impossible to see anything.

But he kept going. Taking one step at a time. Moving his hands along the wall.

He went around a corner. He went around another corner. He came to some stairs. He went up.

There was a door. He pushed against it. Annie pushed too. This door wouldn't budge either.

Was this the same door they had started at?

It was no use. They were trapped.

Annie took his hand in the dark. She squeezed it.

They stood together at the top of the stairs. Listening to the silence.

"*Meow.*"

"Oh, man," Jack whispered.

"He's back!" said Annie.

"*Meow.*"

"Follow him!" cried Jack. "He's going
away from us."

They started down the dark hallway. Following the cat's meow.

Hands against the wall, Jack and Annie stumbled through the darkness.

"Meow."

They followed the sound. All the way through the winding hallway. Down, down, down.

Around one corner, then another. And another...

Finally they saw a light at the end of the tunnel. They rushed forward—out into the bright sunlight.

"Yay!" Annie shouted.

But Jack was thinking.

"Annie," he said. "How did we get out of the false passage?"

"The cat," said Annie.

"But how could the cat do it?" asked Jack.

"Magic," said Annie.

Jack frowned. "But—"

"Look!" said Annie. She pointed.

The cat was bounding away. Over the sand.

"Thank you!" called Annie.

"Thanks!" Jack shouted at the cat.

His black tail waved.

Then he disappeared in the shimmering waves of heat.

Jack looked toward the palm trees. At the top of one sat the tree house. Like a bird's nest.

"Time to go home," Jack said.

He and Annie set off for the palm trees. It was a long hot walk back.

At last Annie grabbed onto the rope ladder. Then Jack.

Once they were inside the tree house, Jack reached for the book about Pennsylvania.

Just then he heard a rumbling sound. The same sound they had heard in the pyramid.

"Look!" Annie said, pointing out the window.

Jack looked.

A boat was beside the pyramid. It was gliding over the sand. Like a boat sailing over the sea.

Then it faded away. Into the distance.

Was it just a mirage?

Or was the ghost-queen finally on her way to the Next Life?

"Home, Jack," whispered Annie.

Jack opened the Pennsylvania book.

He pointed to the picture of Frog Creek.

"I wish we could go home," he said.

The wind began to blow.

The leaves began to shake.

The wind blew harder. It whistled louder.

The tree house started to spin.

It spun faster and faster.

Then everything was still.

Absolutely silent.

10

Another Clue

Late-morning sunlight shone through the tree house window. Shadows danced on the walls and ceiling.

Jack took a deep breath. He was lying on the floor of the tree house.

"I wonder what Mom's making for lunch," said Annie. She was looking out the window.

Jack smiled. Lunch. Mom. Home. It all sounded so real. So calm and safe.

"I hope. it's peanut butter and jelly sand-wiches," he said.

He closed his eyes. The wood floor felt cool.

"Boy, this place is a mess," said Annie. "We'd better make it neater. In case M comes back."

Jack had almost forgotten about M.

Would they ever meet the mysterious M? The person who seemed to own all the books in the tree house?

"Let's put the Egypt book on the bottom of the pile," said Annie.

"Good idea," said Jack. He needed a rest before he visited any more ancient tombs.

"Let's put the dinosaur book on top of the Egypt book," said Annie.

"Yeah, good," said Jack. And a *long* rest before he visited another Tyrannosaurus rex.

"The castle book can go on the very top of the pile," said Annie.

Jack nodded and smiled. He liked thinking about the knight on the cover of the castle book. He felt as if the knight were his friend.

"Jack," said Annie. "Look!"

Jack opened his eyes. She was pointing at the wooden floor.

"What is it?" he asked.

"You have to see for yourself."

Jack groaned as he got up. He stood next to Annie and looked at the floor. He didn't see anything.

"Turn your head a little," said Annie. "You have to catch the light just right."

Jack tipped his head to one side. Something was shining on the floor.

He tipped his head a bit more. A letter came into focus.

The letter M! It shimmered in the sunlight.

This proved the tree house belonged to M.

Absolutely for sure. No question. No doubt about it.

Jack touched the M with his finger. His skin tingled.

Just then the leaves trembled. The wind picked up.

"Let's go down now," he said.

Jack grabbed his backpack. Then he and Annie climbed down the ladder.

As they stood on the ground below the tree house, Jack heard a sound in the bushes.

"Who's there?" he called.

The woods grew still.

"I'm going to bring the medallion back soon," Jack said loudly. "And the bookmark, too. Both of them. Tomorrow!"

"Who are you talking to?" asked Annie.

"I feel like M is nearby," Jack whispered.

Annie's eyes grew wide. "Should we look

for him?"

But just then their mother's voice came from the distance. "Ja-ack! An-nie!"

Jack and Annie looked around at the trees. Then they looked at each other.

"Tomorrow," they said together.

And they took off, running out of the woods.

They ran down their street.

They ran across their yard.

They ran into their house.

They ran into their kitchen.

They ran right into their mom.

She was making peanut butter and jelly sandwiches.

Pirates
Past Noon

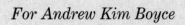

For Andrew Kim Boyce

Contents

1

Too Late!

Jack stared out his bedroom window. The rain kept falling. And falling.

"The TV said it would stop by noon," said Annie, his seven-year-old sister.

"It's already past noon," said Jack.

"But we have to go the tree house," said Annie. "I have a feeling the M person will be there today."

Jack pushed his glasses into place and took a deep breath. He wasn't sure he was ready to meet the M person yet. The mysterious person who had put all the books in the magic tree house.

"Come on," said Annie.

Jack sighed. "Okay," he said. "You get our raincoats and boots. I'll get the medallion and bookmark."

Annie ran to get their rain gear.

Jack reached into his drawer. He took out the medallion.

It was gold. The letter M was engraved on it.

Then he took out the bookmark. It was made of blue leather. It had the same M on it.

Both M's matched the M that was on the floor of the tree house.

Jack put the medallion and bookmark into his backpack. Then he threw in his notebook and pencil. Jack liked to take notes about important things.

"I got our rain stuff!" called Annie.

Jack picked up his pack and went downstairs. Annie was waiting by the back door. She was putting on her boots. "Meet you outside," she said.

Jack pulled on his raincoat and boots. Then he put on his backpack and joined her.

The wind was blowing hard.

"Ready! Set! Go!" shouted Annie.

They kept their heads down and charged into the rainy wind.

Soon they were in the Frog Creek woods.

Tree branches swayed, flinging rainwater everywhere.

"Yuck!" said Annie.

They splashed through puddles. Until they came to the tallest oak tree in the woods.

They looked up.

Tucked between two branches was the tree house. It looked dark and lonely against the stormy sky.

Hanging from the tree house was a rope ladder. It was blowing in the wind.

Jack thought of all the books up there. He hoped they weren't getting wet.

"The M person's been there," said Annie.

Jack caught his breath. "How can you tell?" he said.

"I can feel it," she whispered.

She grabbed the rope ladder and started up. Jack followed.

Inside the tree house it was chilly and damp.

But the books were dry. They were all neatly stacked along the wall. Just the way they had been the day before.

Annie picked up a castle book on top of

one stack. It had taken them to the time of castles.

"Remember the knight?" she said.

Jack nodded. He would never forget the knight who had helped them.

Annie put down the castle book. She picked up the next book on the stack.

It was the dinosaur book that had taken them to the time of dinosaurs.

"Remember?" she said.

Jack nodded.

He'd never forget the pteranodon who had saved him from the Tyrannosaurus rex.

Then Annie held up a book about ancient Egypt.

"Meow," she said.

Jack smiled. The Egypt book had taken them to the time of pyramids. A black cat had come to the rescue there.

"And here's the book about home," Annie said.

She held up the book with the picture of their hometown in it.

Frog Creek, Pennsylvania.

Jack smiled again. The Pennsylvania book had brought them back home at the end of each of their adventures.

Jack sighed. Okay. He still had two main questions.

Who was the M person who had put all the books here?

And did the knight, the pteranodon, and the cat all know the M person?

Finally Jack reached into his backpack. He took out the gold medallion and the leather bookmark. He placed them on the floor. Right over the spot where the M glowed faintly in the wood.

Rain blew into the tree house.

"Brr!" said Annie. "It's not very cozy today."

Jack agreed with her. It was too wet and cold.

"Look." Annie pointed to an open book lying in the corner. "I don't remember a book being open."

"Me neither," said Jack.

Annie picked up the book. She stared at the picture on the page.

"Wow, this place looks great." She showed the picture to Jack.

He saw a sunny beach. A big green parrot sitting in a palm tree. And a ship sailing on a blue sea.

Another gust of rainy wind blew into the tree house.

Annie pointed to the picture. "I wish we

were there instead of here," she said.

"Yeah," said Jack. "But where is there?"

"Too late!" came a squawk.

Jack and Annie turned quickly.

Sitting on a branch outside the window ledge of the tree house was a green parrot. Exactly like the parrot in the picture.

"Too late!" the parrot squawked again.

"A talking parrot!" said Annie. "Is your name Polly? Can I call you Polly?"

Suddenly the wind started to whistle.

"Oh no! Now we're in big trouble!" said Jack.

The wind blew harder.

The leaves shook.

The tree house started to spin. Faster and faster!

Jack squeezed his eyes shut. Then everything was still.

Absolutely still.

Jack opened his eyes.

"Too late!" squawked Polly.

2

The Bright Blue Sea

Jack felt hot sunlight streaming into the tree house.

He smelled saltwater.

He heard the sound of waves.

He and Annie looked out the window.

The tree house was in a palm tree. Beyond was a bright blue sea. A tall sailing ship was on the horizon. It was just like the picture in the book.

"Too late!" squawked Polly.

"Look!" said Annie.

Polly was flying in circles above the tree

house. Then she swooped down to the ocean.

"Come on, let's follow her! Let's go in the water!" said Annie. She took off her raincoat and dropped it on the floor.

"Wait, we have to study the book first," said Jack. He started to reach for the book. But Annie grabbed it.

"You can read it on the beach," she said. Without even looking at the cover, she shoved the book into Jack's backpack.

He sighed. Actually, the water *did* look wonderful.

"Okay," Jack said. He took off his raincoat too.

"Come on!" Annie handed Jack his backpack, then started down the ladder.

Jack folded the raincoat and put it next to the stack of books. He put on his backpack. Then he went down the ladder.

As soon as Annie hit the sand, she ran toward the ocean. Jack watched her wade into the water. She was still wearing her rain boots.

"Your boots, Annie," called Jack.

She shrugged. "They'll dry out," she said.

Jack took off his boots and socks. He put them beside his pack. Then he rolled up his jeans. And ran across the hot sand into the waves.

The water was warm and clear. Jack could see shells and tiny fishes.

He shielded his eyes against the sun. And peered out at the sea.

The tall sailing ship seemed a bit closer.

"Where's Polly?" said Annie.

Jack glanced around. No sign of Polly. Not in the palm trees. Not on the sunlit sand. Not over the bright blue sea.

When Jack looked out at the sea again, the ship seemed even closer. Now Jack could see its flag.

As he stared at the ship's flag, a chill went through him.

The flag was black. *With a skull and crossbones*.

"Oh man," he breathed. He started out of the water.

"What's wrong?" said Annie. She splashed after him.

Jack ran to his backpack. Annie followed.

He grabbed the book from his backpack. He looked at the cover. For the first time, he and Annie read the title of the book.

"Yikes!" said Annie.

"*Pirates of the Caribbean*," Jack read aloud.

3

Three Men in a Boat

"We've come to the time of pirates!" Jack said.

"Pirates?" squeaked Annie. "Like in *Peter Pan*?"

Jack flipped to the picture that showed the parrot, the sea and the ship.

He read the caption under the picture:

> Three hundred years ago, pirates raided Spanish treasure ships in the Caribbean Sea.

He grabbed his notebook and pencil from his pack. He wrote:

pirates in the Caribbean

He turned to the next page. There was a picture of a pirate flag. He read:

> The skull-and-crossbones flag was called the Jolly Roger.

"Let's go!" said Annie.

"Wait!" said Jack. "I want to make a drawing of the flag."

He propped the pirate book in the sand.

He started drawing the Jolly Roger flag.

"Don't copy the picture in the book," said Annie. "Look at the real thing."

But Jack pushed his glasses into place and kept drawing.

"Jack, some pirates are getting into a row-boat," said Annie.

Jack kept drawing.

"Jack, the boat's leaving the big ship," said Annie.

"What?" Jack looked up.

"Look." Annie pointed.

Jack looked. He saw the rowboat coming toward the shore.

"Run!" said Annie. She started running toward the tree house.

Jack jumped up. His glasses fell off.

"Hurry!" Annie called back to him.

Jack went down on his knees. He felt for his glasses. Where were they?

Jack saw something glinting in the sand. He reached for it. It was his glasses. He snatched them up.

Then he threw his notebook and pencil

into his pack. He put the pack on his back.

He grabbed his boots and his socks. And he took off running.

"Hurry! They're coming!" Annie was at the top of the rope ladder.

Jack looked back at the sea. The pirates were closer to the shore.

Suddenly Jack saw the pirate book. In all the confusion he had forgotten it. It was still propped in the sand.

"Oh man, I forgot the book!" he said. He dropped his socks and boots below the tree house.

"Come on, Jack!" Annie shouted.

"I'll be right back!" Jack called. "I've got to get the book!"

"Jack, forget it!"

But Jack was already running toward the water.

Jack grabbed the book.

"Come back!" Annie shouted.

Jack shoved the book into his backpack.

Suddenly a giant wave carried the rowboat right onto the beach.

"Run, Jack!" shouted Annie.

Three big pirates splashed onto the sand.

They had knives in their teeth.

They had pistols in their belts.

They charged toward Jack.

"Run, Jack, run!" cried Annie.

4

Vile Booty

Jack started to run across the hot sand. He ran as fast as he could.

But the pirates ran faster.

Before Jack knew it, the biggest pirate had grabbed him!

Jack struggled. But the pirate had huge, strong arms. He held on to Jack and laughed a mean, ugly laugh. He had a shaggy black beard. A patch covered one eye.

Jack heard Annie yelling. He saw her coming down the rope ladder.

"Stay where you are!" Jack shouted.

But Annie kept coming. "Leave him alone, you bully!" she cried.

The other two pirates laughed meanly. They were dirty and ragged.

Annie charged up to the biggest pirate. "Let him go!" she said. She hit the pirate with her fist and kicked him.

But the pirate just growled. Then he grabbed her, too. And with his giant hands, he held Jack and Annie as if they were two kittens.

"*No* one escapes Cap'n Bones!" he roared. His breath was terrible.

"Let go!" Annie shouted into his face.

But Cap'n Bones just smiled. All his teeth were black.

Annie fell silent.

Cap'n Bones laughed loudly. Then he turned to the other two.

"Find out what's in their house, you dogs," he said.

"Aye, aye, Cap'n!" they answered. And they started up the ladder to the tree house.

"What do you spy, Pinky?" shouted Cap'n Bones.

"Books, Cap'n!" Pinky shouted down.

"Aghh, books," growled Cap'n Bones. He spit on the sand. "I want gold, you dogs!"

"Dogs are nicer than you," said Annie.

"Shhh," said Jack.

"What about you, Stinky?" Cap'n Bones roared.

"Just books, Cap'n!" shouted Stinky.

"Aghh, books," said Cap'n Bones. He spit on the sand again. "I hate books! Keep looking, dogs! Find me something good!"

Cap'n Bones grabbed Jack's backpack.

"What's in here?" he said.

"Nothing—" Jack quickly opened the pack. "Just paper, a pencil, a book."

"Another book!" roared Cap'n Bones. "That's vile booty!"

A gleeful shriek pierced the air.

Cap'n Bones froze. "What's that?" he shouted.

"Look, Cap'n! Look!"

Pinky leaned out the tree house window. He held the medallion. It glimmered in the sunlight.

Oh brother, thought Jack.

"Throw it down!" cried Cap'n Bones.

"It's not yours!" shouted Annie.

Cap'n Bones dropped Jack and Annie. He caught the medallion as it fell.

"Gold! Gold! Gold!" he cried. Cap'n Bones

threw back his head and laughed horribly.

He grabbed two of his pistols. He shot them into the air. Pinky and Stinky howled like wolves.

5

The Kid's Treasure

Jack and Annie watched in horror.

The gold-greedy pirates seemed to have lost their minds.

Jack nudged Annie. Together they started to back slowly away from the pirates. Toward the tree house.

"Halt!" Cap'n Bones shouted. He aimed his pistols at them. "Not another step, lubbers!"

Jack and Annie froze.

Cap'n Bones grinned his black-toothed grin. "Tell old Bones where the rest is," he growled. "Or prepare to meet thy doom."

"What—what rest?" said Annie.

"The rest of the treasure!" roared Cap'n Bones. "I know it's on this island. I have a map!"

He reached into a belt pouch and pulled out a torn piece of paper. He waved it at Jack and Annie.

"Is that a treasure map?" asked Jack.

"Aye, it's the map telling about Kidd's treasure."

"Which kid's treasure? Not *us* kids," said Annie. "We don't know anything about a kid's treasure."

"Why don't you read the map?" said Jack.

"*You* read it!" Cap'n Bones shoved the map in Jack's face.

Jack stared at the strange marks on the paper.

"What does that mean?" asked Jack.

"What does *what* mean?" asked Cap'n Bones.

"Those words." Jack pointed at the words at the bottom of the map.

"Well, it means..." Cap'n Bones' good eye squinted at the writing. He frowned. He coughed. He rubbed his nose.

"Aw, leave him alone," Pinky growled at Jack.

"You know he can't read," said Stinky.

"Shut up!" Cap'n Bones roared at his men.

"Jack and I can read," Annie piped up.

"Shhh," said Jack.

"Cap'n, make 'em read the map!" said Stinky.

Cap'n Bones gave Jack and Annie a dark look. "Read it," he growled.

"Then will you let us go?" said Jack.

The pirate squinted his good eye. "Aye, lubber. When the treasure's in me hands, I'll let you go."

"Okay," said Jack. "I'll read it to you." He looked at the map. "It says, *The gold doth lie beneath the whale's eye.*"

"Heh?" Cap'n Bones scowled. "What's that supposed to mean, lubber?"

Jack shrugged.

"Hang it! Take 'em back to the ship!" shouted Cap'n Bones. "They can rot there till they're ready to tell us how to find Kidd's treasure!"

Jack and Annie were tossed into the rowboat.

Waves splashed the sides. The sky ahead was dark with thunderclouds. A strong wind had started to blow.

"Row, dogs, row!" said Cap'n Bones.

Pinky and Stinky began rowing toward the big ship.

"Look!" Annie said to Jack. She pointed to the shore.

Polly the parrot was flying over the sand.

"She wants to help us," whispered Annie.

Polly started to fly out over the waves. But the winds were too strong. She turned around and flew back to the island.

6

The Whale's Eye

The rowboat tossed from side to side. The waves were huge. Salty spray stung Jack's eyes. He felt seasick.

"Hold 'er steady!" shouted Cap'n Bones.

He pointed at the sea. "Or we'll be meat for those evil brutes!"

Dark fins cut through the water. *Sharks.* One zoomed right by the boat. Jack could have reached out and touched it.

He shuddered.

Soon the rowboat pulled alongside the ship.

The air was filled with wild fiddle music and bagpipes playing. And Jack heard jeers, shouts, and ugly laughter.

"Hoist 'em aboard!" Cap'n Bones shouted to his men.

Annie and Jack were hauled onto the deck. The ship creaked and moaned. It rolled

from side to side. Ropes flapped and snapped
in the wild wind.

Everywhere they looked, Jack and Annie
saw pirates.

Some were dancing. Some were drinking.
Many were fighting. With swords. Or with
their fists.

"Lock 'em in my cabin!" Cap'n Bones ordered.

A couple of pirates grabbed Jack and Annie. And threw them in the ship's cabin. Then locked the door.

The air inside the cabin was damp and sour-smelling. A shaft of gray light came through a small round window.

"Oh man," said Jack. "We've got to figure out how to get back to the island."

"So we can get into the tree house and go home," said Annie.

"Right." Jack suddenly felt tired. How would they ever get out of this mess?

"We better examine the book," he said.

He reached into his pack and pulled out the pirate book.

He flipped through the pages.

He looked for information to help them.

"Look," he said.

He found a picture of pirates burying a treasure chest. "This might help."

Together they read the words under the picture.

> Captain Kidd was a famous pirate. It is said that he buried a treasure chest on a deserted island. The chest was filled with gold and jewels.

"Captain Kidd!" said Jack.

"So *that's* the *kid* that Bones keeps talking about," said Annie.

"Right," said Jack.

Annie looked out the round window.

"And Captain Kidd's treasure is buried somewhere on the island," she said.

Jack took out his notebook and pencil. He wrote:

Captain Kidd's treasure on island

"Ja-ack," Annie said.

"Shhh, wait a minute," he said. "I'm thinking."

"Guess what I see?" said Annie.

"What?" Jack asked. He looked back at the book.

"A whale."

"Neat," he said. Then he looked up. "A whale? Did you say . . . a whale?"

"A whale. A huge whale. As big as a football field."

Jack jumped up and looked out the window with her.

"Where?" Jack asked. All he could see was the island. And stormy waves. And shark fins.

"There!" said Annie.

"Where? Where?"

"There! The *island* is shaped like a giant whale!"

"Oh man," whispered Jack. Now he could see it.

"See the whale's back?" said Annie.

"Yep." The slope of the island looked like the back of a whale.

"See his spout?" said Annie.

"Yep." The palm tree that held the tree house looked like the spout of the whale.

"See his eye?" said Annie.

"Yep." A big black rock looked like the eye of the whale.

"The gold doth lie beneath the whale's eye," whispered Jack. "Wow."

7

Gale's a-Blowin'

"So the treasure must be under that rock," said Annie.

"Right," said Jack. "Now we just have to get back to the island. We'll show Cap'n Bones where the treasure is. Then while all the pirates are digging, we'll sneak up to the tree house."

"And make a wish to go home," said Annie.

"Right." Jack poked his head out of the round window of the cabin. "Cap'n Bones, sir!" he shouted.

The pirates took up the cry. "Cap'n Bones! Cap'n Bones!"

"Hey?" came a horrible voice.

Cap'n Bones stuck his ugly face through the window. His good eye glared at Jack. "What do you want, lubbers?"

"We're ready to tell the truth, sir," said Jack.

"Go ahead," growled Cap'n Bones.

"We know where Captain Kidd's treasure is."

"Where?"

"We can't just tell you. We have to *show* you," said Annie.

Cap'n Bones gave Annie and Jack a long hard look.

"You'll need a rope," said Jack.

"And shovels," said Annie.

Cap'n Bones growled. Then he roared at

his men, "Get some rope and shovels!"

"Aye, aye, Cap'n!"

"Then throw these lubbers in the boat! We're going back to the island!"

"Aye, aye, Cap'n!"

Back in the rowboat, Jack saw the sky had grown even darker with clouds. The waves were bigger. The wind was howling.

"Gale's a-blowin'!" said Pinky.

"You'll see a gale if I don't get me gold today, by thunder!" Cap'n Bones shouted. "Row, dogs, row!"

The three pirates battled the waves, until the rowboat reached the island. They all piled onto the shore.

Cap'n Bones grabbed Jack and Annie.

"Okay, lubbers," he said. "Now show us where the treasure is."

"There," said Annie. She pointed at the

black rock near the tip of the island.

"Under that rock," said Jack.

Cap'n Bones dragged Jack and Annie down the beach to the black rock.

"Get to work!" Cap'n Bones said to Pinky and Stinky.

"What about you?" said Annie.

"Me? Work?" Cap'n Bones chuckled.

Jack gulped. How could they get away from him?

"Don't you think you should help your friends?" he said.

Cap'n Bones gave Jack a horrible grin. "Nay. I'm going to hold you two—till there's treasure in me hands!"

8

Dig, Dogs, Dig

Pinky and Stinky tied their rope around the big rock.

The wind howled. The two pirates pulled. And pulled. And pulled.

"They need help!" said Jack.

"Aghh, let the dogs do the work!" growled Cap'n Bones.

"You're not very nice to them," said Annie.

"Who cares?" roared Cap'n Bones.

"Cap'n! We got it!" shouted Pinky.

They started pulling the rock across the sand.

"Now let's dig where the rock was," said Jack. "All of us!"

But Cap'n Bones ignored his suggestion.

"Dig, you dogs!" he shouted.

Pinky and Stinky started to dig. The wind blew even harder. There was going to be a thunderstorm.

"Oww! I got sand in me eyes!" Pinky whined.

"Oww! Me back hurts!" Stinky cried.

"Dig!" shouted Cap'n Bones. He held Jack and Annie with one hand. With the other he pulled out the gold medallion.

He tossed it at the two pirates. It fell into the hole.

"Dig for more of these, you swine!" he said.

Squawk!

"Look!" Annie said.

Polly was back! She was circling above them!

"Go back!" she squawked.

275

Stinky and Pinky looked up at the parrot. They scowled.

"Dig!" shouted Cap'n Bones.

"A big storm is comin', Cap'n!" said Pinky.

"Go back!" said Polly.

"The bird's an omen, Cap'n!" shouted Stinky.

"Dig, you dogs!" cried Cap'n Bones.

"Go back!" squawked Polly.

"The bird's warning us!" shouted Pinky. "We've got to get to the ship before it's too late!"

The two pirates threw down their shovels. They started running toward the rowboat.

"Mutineers! Come back!" shouted Cap'n Bones. He dragged Jack and Annie down the beach as he ran after his men. "Stop!"

But the pirates kept running. They got to the rowboat and pushed it into the sea.

"Wait!" cried Cap'n Bones.

Pinky and Stinky jumped into the boat. They started rowing.

"Wait!" Cap'n Bones let go of Jack and Annie. He ran into the water. "Wait, you dogs!"

He hauled himself into the rowboat.

Then the three pirates disappeared into the spray of the waves.

"Go back!" squawked Polly.

"She means *us*!" said Annie.

Just then the storm broke over the island. The wind howled. Rain fell in buckets.

"Let's go!" cried Annie.

"Wait! I have to get the medallion!" shouted Jack. He ran to the hole dug by the pirates. He looked down in it.

Even in the dreary light, the medallion was shining.

Big, fat raindrops were falling into the hole, washing away the sand.

Jack saw a patch of wood.

Then the rain cleared away more sand. And Jack saw the top of an old trunk.

He stared. Was it Captain Kidd's treasure chest?

"Hurry, Jack!" cried Annie. She was half-way up the tree house ladder.

"I found it! I found it!" cried Jack. "I found the treasure chest!"

"Forget the treasure chest!" said Annie. "We have to go now! The storm's getting worse!"

Jack kept staring at the chest. Was there gold inside? Silver? Precious gems?

"Come on!" Now Annie was shouting from the tree house window.

But Jack couldn't tear himself away. He

brushed the rest of the muddy sand off the chest.

"Jack, forget the treasure chest!" cried Annie. "Let's go!"

"Go back!" squawked Polly.

Jack looked at the parrot. She was perched on the black rock.

He stared into her wise eyes. He thought he knew her—knew her from somewhere else.

"Go back, Jack," she said. She sounded like a person.

Okay. It was definitely time to go.

Jack took one last look at the treasure chest. He clutched the gold medallion. Then he took off, running toward the tree house.

His socks and rain boots were still there. He quickly pulled the boots on. He shoved the socks into his backpack.

The rope ladder was dancing wildly in the wind. Jack grabbed it.

The ladder swayed as Jack climbed. He was tossed this way and that. But he held on tight.

At last he pulled himself into the tree house.

"Let's go!" he cried.

Annie was already holding the Pennsylvania book. She pointed to the picture of Frog Creek.

"I wish we could go there!" she shouted.

The wind was already blowing hard. But now it blew even harder.

The tree house started to spin. It spun faster and faster.

Then everything was still.

Absolutely still.

9

The Mysterious M

Drip, drip.

Jack opened his eyes.

Rain was dripping from the leaves of the tree.

They were back in Frog Creek. The rain was softer. The wind was gentler. The air was sweeter.

"Oh man." Jack sighed. "That was close." He was still holding the gold medallion.

"Polly's gone," said Annie sadly. "I was hoping she might come back with us."

"No magic creature has ever come back with us," said Jack.

He pulled off his backpack. It was damp with rain and saltwater.

Jack took out the pirate book. He put it on the stack of books. On top of the dinosaur book. And the knight book. And the mummy book.

Then Jack put the gold medallion beside the bookmark with the letter M.

Next he went down onto his knees. And ran his finger over the shimmering M on the floor. "We didn't find any M's on this trip," he said.

"Or the M person," said Annie.

Squawk!

"Polly!" Annie cried.

The parrot swooshed into the tree house.

She perched on the stack of books.

Polly looked straight at Jack.

"What—what are you doing here?" he asked her.

Slowly Polly raised her bright green wings. They grew bigger and bigger until they spread out like a huge green cape.

Then, in a great swirl of colors—in a blur of feathers and light—in a flapping and stretching and screeching—a new being took shape.

Polly was not a parrot any longer. In her place was an old woman. A beautiful old woman with long white hair and piercing eyes.

She wore a green feathered cape. She perched on the stack of books. And she was very calm and very still.

Neither Jack nor Annie could speak. They were too amazed.

"Hello, Jack. Hello, Annie," the old woman said. "My name is Morgan le Fay."

10

Treasure Again

Annie found her voice first. "The M person," she whispered.

"Yes. I'm the M person," said Morgan.

"Wh-where are you from?" asked Jack.

"Have you ever heard of King Arthur?" said Morgan.

Jack nodded.

"Well, I am King Arthur's sister," said Morgan.

"You're from Camelot," said Jack. "I've read about Camelot."

"What did you read about me, Jack?" said Morgan.

"You—you're a witch."

Morgan smiled. "You can't believe *everything* you read, Jack."

"But are you a magician?" said Annie.

"Most call me an enchantress. But I'm also a librarian," said Morgan.

"A librarian?" said Annie.

"Yes. And I've come to the 20th century, your time, to collect books. You are lucky to be born in a time with so many books."

"For the Camelot library?" asked Jack.

"Precisely," said Morgan. "I travel in this tree house to collect words from many different places around the world. And from many different time periods."

"Did you find books here?" said Jack.

"Oh yes. Many wonderful books. I want to

borrow them for our scribes to copy."

"Did you put all the bookmarks in them?" said Jack.

"Yes. You see, I like the pictures in the books. Sometimes I want to visit the scenes in the pictures. So all the bookmarks mark places I wish to go."

"How do you get there?" asked Annie.

"I placed a spell on the tree house," said Morgan. "So when I point to a picture and make the wish, the tree house takes me there."

"I think you dropped this in dinosaur times," said Jack.

He handed the gold medallion to Morgan.

"Oh, thank you! I wondered where I'd lost it," she said. She put the medallion into a hidden pocket in her cape.

"So can anybody work the spell?" asked

Annie. "Anybody who tries it?"

"Oh dear, no! Not just anybody," Morgan said. "You two are the only ones besides me to do it. No one else has ever even seen my tree house before."

"Is it invisible?" asked Annie.

"Yes," said Morgan. "I had no idea it would ever be discovered. But then you two came along. Somehow you hooked right into my magic."

"H-how?" asked Jack.

"Well, for two reasons, I think," explained Morgan. "First, Annie believes in magic. So she actually saw the tree house. And her belief helped you to see it, Jack."

"Oh man," said Jack.

"Then you picked up a book, Jack. And because you love books so much, you caused my magic spell to work."

"Wow," said Annie.

"You can't imagine my dismay when you started to take off for dinosaur times. I had to make a very quick decision. And I decided to come along."

"Oh, so you were the pteranodon!" said Annie.

Morgan smiled.

"And the cat and the knight and Polly!" said Annie.

"Yes," said Morgan softly.

"You were all these things to help us?" asked Jack.

"Yes, but I must go home now. The people in Camelot need my help."

"You're leaving?" whispered Jack.

"I'm afraid I must," said Morgan.

She picked up Jack's backpack and handed it to him. Jack and Annie picked up their raincoats. It had stopped raining.

"You won't forget us, will you?" asked Annie, as they put their raincoats on.

"Never," said Morgan. She smiled at both of them. "You remind me too much of myself. You love the impossible, Annie. And you love knowledge, Jack. What better combination is there?"

Morgan le Fay touched Annie's forehead gently. And then Jack's. She smiled.

"Good-bye," she said.

"Good-bye," said Annie and Jack.

Annie left the tree house first. Jack followed. They climbed down the rope ladder for the last time.

They stood below the oak tree and looked up.

Morgan was looking out the window. Her long white hair blew in the breeze.

Suddenly the wind began to blow.

The leaves began to shake.

A loud whistling sound filled the air.

Jack covered his ears and squeezed his eyes shut.

Then everything was silent.

Absolutely silent.

Jack opened his eyes.

The tree house was gone.

All gone.

Absolutely gone.

Annie and Jack stood a moment, staring up at the empty oak tree. Listening to the silence.

Annie sighed. "Let's go," she said softly.

Jack just nodded. He felt too sad to speak. As they started walking, he put his hands into his pockets.

He felt something.

Jack pulled out the gold medallion. "Look!"

he said. "How did—?"

Annie smiled. "Morgan must have put it there," she said.

"But how?"

"Magic," said Annie. "I think it means she'll be coming back."

Jack smiled. He clutched the medallion as he and Annie took off through the wet, sunny woods.

As they walked, the sun shined through the woods. And all the wet leaves sparkled.

Everything, in fact, was shining.

Leaves, branches, puddles, bushes, grass, vines, wild flowers—all glittered like jewels.

Or gleamed like gold.

Annie had been right, thought Jack.

Forget the treasure chest.

They had treasure at home. A ton of it. Everywhere.

**Are you ready
for more adventures
with Jack and Annie?**

Read the next four
Magic Tree House books
and join the
Magic Tree House Club!

The Magic Tree House is back…but Morgan has disappeared! Find out the secret of Morgan's spell when you read the next four Magic Tree House books.

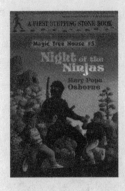

Magic Tree House #5, NIGHT OF THE NINJAS, in which Jack and Annie go to old Japan and learn the ways of the ninjas.

Magic Tree House #6, AFTERNOON ON THE AMAZON, in which Jack and Annie explore the wild rain forest of the Amazon and are greeted by giant ants, hungry crocodiles, and flesh-eating piranhas.

Magic Tree House #7, SUNSET OF THE SABERTOOTH, in which Jack and Annie go back to the Ice Age—the world of woolly mammoths, sabertooth tigers, and a mysterious sorcerer.

And coming in Fall 1996— **Magic Tree House #8,** MIDNIGHT ON THE MOON, in which Jack and Annie step into the future and onto the moon.

Do you love the Magic Tree House books?

Climb the ladder into
The Magic Tree House Club!

You'll get:
- three newsletters in a year filled with fun facts, games, puzzles, and a note from author Mary Pope Osborne
- a super Magic Tree House poster
- plus chances to win free books and prizes

- -

SIGN ME UP! I want to be a member of
The Magic Tree House Club.

MY NAME: _____

MY ADDRESS: _____

_____

Have an adult write a $1.50 check or money order payable to Random House, Inc. for shipping and handling. Send this coupon and your check or money order to:

> The Magic Tree House Club
> Random House, Inc.
> 201 East 50th Street
> Mail Drop 30-2
> New York, NY 10022

About the Author

Mary Pope Osborne visits schools all over the country and talks to students about her Magic Tree House books. "Kids are a great help to me," she says. "I always get them to vote on where they think Jack and Annie should go. Lots of kids even write their own Magic Tree House stories and share them with me."

If you'd like to share *your* Magic Tree House ideas with Ms. Osborne, you can write to her at this address:

> Magic Tree House Series
> c/o Random House, Inc.
> Mail Drop 28-2
> 201 East 50th Street
> New York, NY 10022

If you loved reading the Magic Tree House books, try these other Random House titles:

FIRST STEPPING STONES

The Houdini Club Magic Mystery series
BY DAVID ADLER
Onion Sundaes
Wacky Jacks

BY KATHLEEN LEVERICH
Brigid Bewitched
Brigid Beware
Brigid the Bad

BY BARBARA PARK
Junie B. Jones and the Stupid Smelly Bus (#1)
Junie B. Jones and a Little Monkey Business (#2)
Junie B. Jones and Her Big Fat Mouth (#3)
Junie B. Jones and Some Sneaky Peeky Spying (#4)
Junie B. Jones and the Yucky Blucky Fruitcake (#5)
Junie B. Jones and That Meanie Jim's Birthday (#6)

BY LOUIS SACHAR
Marvin Redpost: Kidnapped at Birth
Marvin Redpost: Why Pick on Me?
Marvin Redpost: Is He a Girl?
Marvin Redpost: Alone in His Teacher's House

The Genghis Kahn, Dog Star series
BY MARJORIE WEINMAN SHARMAT
The Great Genghis Khan Look-Alike Contest (#1)
Genghis Kahn: A Dog Star Is Born (#2)
Genghis Kahn: Dog-Gone Hollywood (#3)

Tooter Pepperday BY JERRY SPINELLI
Ginger Brown: Too Many Houses BY SHARON DENNIS WYETH
Tamika and the Wisdom Rings BY CAMILLE YARBROUGH

STEPPING STONES

The Adventures of Ratman BY ELLEN WEISS AND
MEL FRIEDMAN
Aliens for Breakfast BY JONATHAN ETRA AND
STEPHANIE SPINNER
Aliens for Lunch BY JONATHAN ETRA AND STEPHANIE SPINNER
Aliens for Dinner BY STEPHANIE SPINNER
The Chalk Box Kid BY CLYDE ROBERT BULLA
Great-Uncle Dracula BY JAYNE HARVEY
Howie Merton and the Magic Dust BY FAYE COUCH REEVES
Julian, Secret Agent BY ANN CAMERON
The Mystery of Pony Hollow BY LYNN HALL
Next Spring an Oriole BY GLORIA WHELAN
Night of the Full Moon BY GLORIA WHELAN
Pioneer Cat BY WILLIAM H. HOOKS
Silver BY GLORIA WHELAN
Slime Time BY JIM AND JANE O'CONNOR
Star BY JO ANN SIMON
White Bird BY CLYDE ROBERT BULLA

BULLSEYE STEP INTO CLASSICS™

BULLSEYE CHILLERS™